Doreen,
Enjoy!

TRAFFICKED DREAMS

INSPECTOR BRIANA RYU SERIES

BOOK 1

HEATHER OSBORNE

COPYRIGHT 2020 BY HEATHER OSBORNE

This is a work of fiction. Names, characters, places, and incidents are either the product of the author's imagination or used fictitiously and any resemblance to actual people, alive or dead, business, establishments, locales, or events is entirely coincidental.

Any reference to real events, businesses, or organizations is intended to give the fiction a sense of realism and authenticity.

All rights reserved. No part of this publication may be reproduced, stored in a retrieval system, or transmitted by any means—electronic, mechanical, photographic (photocopying), recording or otherwise—without prior permission in writing from the author.

Any errors are the sole responsibility of the author.

Cover Design by Heather Osborne
Editing by Susie Watson

ISBN: 9798646131837
Independently published

DEDICATION

To the survivors of human trafficking, and to the people who work effortlessly to help them.

And to my grandfather. I miss you every day.

1
LINA

Every limb in my body aches. I want to cry, but dehydration has removed that option. I lie as still as possible on the bed, hoping it will envelop me. The door creaks open, and I want to jump up; run away. Fighting has just made the situation so much worse.

"Lina?"

Max's voice finds my ears, and the tension dissipates.

"Lina, are you in here?" He's frantically whispering.

I manage a moan, and he winds his way through the beds to my side. He takes my hand, and I can see his face in the dim light.

"What happened?"

I shake my head, not knowing if he can see the movement. "Oh, Max, we made a mistake."

Max squeezes my hand. "I know…they have me delivering drugs. And if I don't get the money they need, they hit and starve me."

I don't want to tell him what they do to women.

"I can get away…find help…but I don't know how to get back here. They blindfold me."

"Anything is better than this."

A thump sounds from outside the door.

"You have to go. If they find you here, they will kill…"

The door swings open, and Max dives beneath my bed.

I pray he covers his ears, so he doesn't hear what happens next.

2

The deserted Embarcadero BART terminal stank of urine and rotten food. Inspector Briana Ryu wrinkled her nose at the stench, even though she used the Bay Area Rapid Transit service nearly every day to commute from South San Francisco into the city. It wasn't ideal, but it sure as hell beat paying the extortionate parking fees. She adjusted her distressed brown leather messenger bag on her shoulder, checking that she'd taken off her badge before she'd left the station. Nothing attracted unwanted attention faster than a flash of shiny metal on black leather.

"Shit." Her fingers brushed over the badge attached to her waistband. Casting a quick look around, she unclipped it from her belt and swung the bag around to tuck it away. As her attention was elsewhere, Bri didn't see the small figure approach until the tiny hand encircled her wrist.

She jumped, snatching her hand back reflexively. The figure recoiled, large blue eyes darting back and forth, as if rethinking an escape route. Assessing the situation, Bri skimmed her own dark eyes over the pitiful child before her. He couldn't have been much more than twelve years old, wearing ripped jeans and a torn dirty T-shirt. His blond hair was filthy.

"Sorry, I…"

Before she could continue, the boy interrupted. "Help me…please."

Bri scanned the area again, searching for any other adult or a transit police officer. It was nearly eleven at night, and commuters at this hour were rare. "Are you lost?"

The boy shook his head. "Please, can we leave?" His accent didn't sound like he was from the area, but then again, she'd been surprised before. He frantically glanced over his shoulder.

Bri inwardly groaned. She had just worked a twelve-hour shift and wanted nothing more than to go home to her small apartment and heat up a T.V. dinner. However, something in the kid's eyes made her take pause. He had the haunted expression of someone who had seen horrific things.

The announcement sounded for her train, and she made a quick decision. "Sure, uh, come on."

The boy stuck to her side as they ascended from the underground transport system to the main street. Bri glanced down at him, shivering in his thin T-shirt. The pair exchanged no more words as she headed back to the San Francisco Police Department Central Station on Vallejo Street, crossing through reception with a nod to the desk sergeant, who raised an eyebrow with a curious frown. Bri shook her head, guiding the young child up to the Personal Crimes division in the Investigations Department.

Inspector William 'Billy' Trent caught her eye as she approached. "Thought you were callin' it. Who's this?"

Bri shrugged. "Found me in the BART station. Do me a favor, get him a blanket and something to drink. Maybe put him in the family room? I gotta talk to the Cap and see about getting social work on the horn…"

"No!" The kid backed into the desk with such force, it rattled Trent's coffee mug.

"Whoa, calm down." Bri held out her hands in a placating manner. They were drawing the attention of a few other officers who had remained for night shift.

"No…they don't listen…they are…" The kid started hyperventilating.

"Shit. Trent, get the Cap." Reaching out, Bri hesitantly put her hand on the boy's shoulder. "Calm down. What if I take you to the family room? Would that be okay?"

The boy's eyes skidded over the rows of desks, and finally, he nodded. Bri dumped her messenger bag on her desk chair as she led him over to the small room they kept for interviewing sensitive case victims. She opened the door and flicked on the light, struck by how stark the furnishings were.

"You want a Coke, or something else?"

The boy shook his head, eyes darting like captured prey. He finally sat on one of the sofas, watching Bri.

"So, what's your name?"

"Maksym…but people call me Max." The accent became more profound when he said his name.

"And where are you from, Max?"

Trent entered the room, causing Max to jolt and sit straight up. "Sorry. I got a blanket and a bottle of water. You hungry?"

Max nodded eagerly.

"Right, McDonald's?"

Another nod and maybe a faint smile of longing.

Trent met Bri's look. "I'll be back in a bit. The Cap'll be in shortly."

Once the door had closed again, Bri smiled at Max. Her thoughts ran wild, wondering about this skinny boy who had asked her for help. "Where are you from?" she repeated.

"Ukraine."

Bri sighed, knowing she should have Trent call social work, despite the boy's reaction…or even the blasted Immigration and Customs Enforcement. However, she couldn't resist the opportunity to press on with questioning before the Feds took over. "And how did you get to San Francisco, Max?"

The boy studied his dirt-rimmed fingernails. "A man came to our city. He met my sister where she worked, promised her marriage and many fine things. Our parents died when we were young, and she took care of me."

"Your English is very good."

"We studied hard when he said he would take both of us to America. My sister, Lina, she wouldn't leave without me."

Bri glanced up as Trent opened the door, trying to ignore how the boy jumped at the squeak from the old wood. The scent of French fries and burgers wafted in, and she could have sworn Max wiped drool off his chin. As Trent handed over the bag, he dug into it, scoffing the food as if he hadn't seen nutrition in days.

"When was the last time you ate?"

"Oh, I don't know…maybe two days ago? There was punishment."

"Punishment?" Internally, Bri admonished herself again. She should wait for a trained officer in child interviews; she should call social work. Lots of 'shoulds' she pushed out of her mind for the moment.

"If we do not get the girls to enough men, or make enough money with the drugs, they punish us."

Bri was aware of human trafficking going on in the city. It wasn't unheard of in such a densely populated area. No doubt a perfect base for these criminals who sold people like cattle. There had been recent busts of rings, but the traffickers got smarter, transporting their victims to different cities. Keeping track of them was a huge task, and often, it got lost in the other, less complicated (for lack of a better word), crimes. They'd report their suspicions to the FBI and usually let the Feds take it from there.

"Max, where is your sister now?"

He shook his head, mouth full of masticated meat. "Don't know. They took her last night in a van. They drug the women, so they don't resist."

There was a knock at the door, and Bri stood. "I'll be right back."

Captain Bradley Meyers stood outside the room; his face set in a hard frown. "Come on, Ryu, you know you shouldn't be in there."

"Sorry, Cap, but I thought I could get some preliminary facts out of him…like if his sister was in immediate danger."

"The drill is we report to social work. They take it from there. I've already made the call."

Bri cursed under her breath. "The kid was adamant. He didn't want to talk with anyone in that sector. We were building a rapport, and…" A slamming sound from inside the room caught their attention. She pushed open the door, and the room was empty. "Shit!"

She crossed the room to the window, the glass still shuddering. She opened it and looked down the fire escape. "Hey!" she called out at the shadowy figure fleeing down the steps at an alarming rate. "Hey, come back!"

Her shouts were useless. He was gone.

3

Six Months Later

Bri laughed as she circled the unmarked car, getting into the driver seat. The Wednesday night shift was just beginning, and she hoped for an easy ride. "Trent, you're nuts."

Her partner chuckled in response, giving her a helpless shrug. "What? You don't think Christine will like it?"

Trent had been on and off for years with his girlfriend, Christine. When the couple wasn't fighting, they resembled teenagers, unable to get enough of each other. Bri couldn't comprehend the relationship. How could you be involved in something so unpredictable and volatile?

"I think she's going to screw your brains out, like she does every time you give her something expensive. Is this making up for leaving your socks on her pillow the other week?"

"Naw, this time it's for shrinking her cashmere sweater in the dryer."

Bri winced. "Ooo, that sucks. Didn't you know

cashmere is dry clean only?"

"I know now. She tried to shove the doll-sized thing over my head." Trent rubbed his ear. "I think she bruised my brain."

"Serves you right." Bri started the car, pulling slowly into traffic on the Embarcadero. The sun was fading in the sky as they began their second night shift in a row. The early November sky grayed. "Looks like rain."

"Yup, we could use it too. Drought's been hell this year."

As if on cue, the patter of rain began to pelt their car as they cruised along back to the station. Trent had had a craving for Bubba Gump's, so they had grabbed a bite to eat at Pier 39 before heading in. He'd picked her up at the BART station, but Bri always insisted on driving, something about Trent being a maniac in the tight traffic around the city. The pair worked in Central District of the SFPD, mainly comprising of the Financial District, Chinatown, North Beach, and Fisherman's Warf. They also covered Telegraph, Nob, and Russian Hills. Their beat was in the heart of the City, and full of tourists.

"Car 227, over." Dispatch had their radio humming to life.

Trent answered, leaving Bri to navigate the idiots who didn't signal when changing lanes. "Yup, this is Car 227, over."

"Suspected 187 in North Beach on Powell Street. What's your location?"

"ETA twenty minutes, depending on traffic, 10-4." Trent replaced the radio. "Suspected homicide."

"Yeah, I can hear. So much for a quiet night." She aimed the car in the direction of the call as the rain thrummed on the windshield.

They pulled up at the end of the street, uniformed patrols having already cordoned off the area and keeping back the few people who had ventured out into the

9

inclement weather to observe the events. Huddling in her jacket, Bri advanced to the yellow tape, flashing her badge. The uniform let her and Trent past, recording their names on his log. The rain dripped off the plastic protector on his hat. "Over there...behind the school."

Bri nodded and advanced, her boots squelching in the puddles. The medical examiner, Dr. Catriona Hayes, held up a hand as her suited colleagues continued to comb the scene for evidence. After a series of photographs and gathering of any evidence not washed away by the rain, she beckoned them under the tent.

"Juvenile, aged ten to fourteen. I'll know more once I get him on the table. Poor kid. I hate these cases."

"Don't we all, Cat?" Bri had known Dr. Hayes since she had started as an officer with the department. The two had become fast friends with a strong professional courtesy for each other's work. She liked when Cat was on shift; it made her job that much easier. "Can we have a look?"

Hayes nodded and drew back the tarp, which had protected the body from the rain until they had erected the tent to protect it.

"Shit."

Trent, whose attention had been drawn away by the crowd, refocused on the scene. "What?"

"Recognize him?" Bri knelt, the haunting blue eyes fixed and cloudy. His blond hair was dirty and matted with blood.

He frowned and shook his head. "Can't say I do, Bri. Who is it?"

"The kid from the precinct...about six months ago now. Remember? You bought him McDonald's?"

"Shit," Trent echoed Bri's sentiments. "You sure?"

"Yeah, it's the eyes. You don't forget a thing like that... I think his name was Max, but that was a nickname. She closed her eyes, rifling through her memories. "Maksym, that's it."

"Last name?"

"He never said. His sister was called Lina. They were brought here from Ukraine."

"Think ICE will have anything on them?"

Bri stood, rubbing her lower back. "No, they were undoubtably trafficked into the country, if I remember what he said before the Cap scared him off with the threat of social work."

Trent shook his head. "No tact. Asshole. Always thought he was better than us."

"Hey, can we leave the disgruntled public servant act for a moment? I gotta get this kid out of the rain before we lose everything."

Bri and Trent stepped back, allowing Hayes to direct the removal of the body. Bri did a slow circuit around the concealed alcove behind the school, looking up at the glowing lights in the apartments above the shops, wondering if anyone had seen or heard anything. Making her way back to Trent, she touched his arm. "Billy, we need to question the people around this block. Let's make a start."

Hayes paused at the back of the van. "Bri, you should know something."

She hurried over to her side. "What's up?" Bri leaned on the van door, her eyes flitting over the black body bag.

"He was dumped, I'd bet my scalpel on it."

"What makes you think that?"

"I've seen this type of dump before. Fingers cut off, teeth removed. It's vile, but often effective. Someone didn't want this kid to be IDed." Nodding sadly, Hayes hopped out of the back of the van and shut the door, circling around to the passenger side. "Guess it was luck you knew him, eh?"

Bri sighed. "Yeah…luck." The rain trickled under the collar of her jacket as she watched the van pull off into the night.

Trent ambled back over. "Uniforms say the call was anonymous, came in around eight, so we have nothing to go on. I'll take this side; you take that side?"

※ ※ ※

The canvas of the neighborhood surrounding where Max had been found was proving unfruitful. People, on the whole, wanted nothing to do with any type of murder investigation, and Bri was ready to lose her temper when she knocked on the last door, in a house whose window overlooked the alley.

An elderly man opened the door, his back curved with age, but his dark eyes sharp. "Yes?"

Bri held up her badge. "Hi there. We're investigating a situation which may have happened earlier in the evening or even last night. Can I ask you a few questions?"

"Inspector Ryu?" He inspected her badge, widening the door, his face losing the suspicious air people often carried when they were confronted by law enforcement. He also pronounced her last name correctly, as 'You,' not adding the 'R' sound.

She nodded, surprise crossing her face.

"You're not full Korean, are you?"

Bri stepped back in semi-shock. "Uh, no, my dad is half, my grandfather was full. My mom is Russian/Irish."

"Did you grow up in the city?" He motioned for her to come in, hobbling back into the living room. The small apartment was exceedingly tidy, and he switched off a small flat-screen television perched on a stand in the corner of the room. Lining the wall above a fake fireplace were rows of family photos—smiling children, weddings, and an aged couple in the middle.

"No, on the outskirts. South City."

"Ah, yes, my grandson lives there. His wife is expecting a baby. My first great-grandchild." Pride blossomed on his lined face as he lowered himself into a chair. "Ah. So, young lady, what can I do to help?"

Bri perched on the edge of a brocade sofa. "I don't know if you've seen what's happening down in the alley…"

"I saw the police lights. I keep to myself, usually. No need to get myself in trouble. My late wife always said I was too nosy for my own good." He smiled sadly at the photograph of a woman sitting on his side table. "My Sarah. I'm Carl Yoong." He pressed a hand to his chest.

"Pleased to meet you. We're just going around asking if anyone heard anything earlier tonight, or maybe last night?"

Mr. Yoong nodded once. "Yes, tonight, but at the time, I didn't think anything of it. Such a racket goes on in that alley sometimes. Dumpsters and all. You know."

Bri withdrew a leather-covered notepad from her jacket pocket. "Could you tell me what you heard, please?"

His eyes looked to the curtained window. "Will I remain anonymous?"

"Of course." Her pen was poised and ready. "Do you know what time it was?"

"Oh, I suppose around eight pm…Wheel of Fortune had ended, and I was considering going to sleep."

Bri checked her watch, noting the time was just after 9:00pm. So, this could be Mr. Yoong hearing the body being left.

"I heard a thump and then the squealing of tires. It's nothing unusual. You know how the kids drive in this city. I went to the window, and saw tail lights heading toward Powell. I didn't think much of it and went back to my programs."

"Thank you, Mr. Yoong, you've been very helpful."

He laughed, a light, throaty sound, before coughing. "Excuse me. I don't think I have been, but I hope you figure out what's going on. May I ask what happened?"

"A boy was found murdered, I'm afraid." Bri felt a connection with this man, something she hadn't felt since her grandfather had passed away the previous year.

Mr. Yoong tsked softly. "So tragic to have a young life ripped away. I always tell my grandchildren to live life to the fullest. Make mistakes, love, laugh, and most of all, stick to family. Family is everything."

Bri inhaled, pushing back the forming tears. "Yes, sir, it is." She stood. "I appreciate your help and…congratulations on your great-grandchild."

He lifted himself up and patted her arm. "Thank you." He ushered her to the door. "Take care of yourself, Inspector Ryu." He smiled warmly and shut the door, leaving her in the hallway.

Bri's body drained of feeling. These were the times she would have gone to speak to her grandfather—trying to unravel the flaws in society and why things happened the way they did. He had told her once that things were going south in California, that there were better opportunities out there for her. But she loved her city and the proximity to her parents and grandparents. Nothing would take her away, so she worked to make a difference in her own small way.

Trent met her at the bottom of the stairs. "Any luck?"

"Not until my last house. A man said he heard noises around eight. Looked and saw a van heading out on Powell."

"Yeah, about the same as what I got from an old lady on the end. She didn't want me to leave. I ended up sitting through two albums of her cat." Trent shifted uncomfortably, running his hand over his brown hair, uncertainty flickering in his hazel eyes. For a man as intimidating and muscular as her partner, he had an unholy fear of felines.

"Poor baby." She lightly punched his arm, and they

headed over to their parked car. "So…timeline wise, we've got an anonymous call at eight to 911, a body recovered around nine, and two confirmations of a van leaving the alleyway at eight."

"What now?"

"I think we're gonna have to consult with a few resources to see which rings are operating out of our area. I know his sister was involved, and he was most likely dragged along. Young kids can come in handy as runners." She groaned. "And we'll have to tell Meyers."

"Joy of joys." Trent sank into the passenger seat. "Not it!"

"You asshole!" Bri grumbled as she started the car. "You owe me."

"Next Bubba's is on me."

"Try the next ten. He likes you." She drove toward the precinct. "He has some grudge against me."

"You're better than him, Ryu. He doesn't like that."

True enough, Bri had a steady string of solved cases in the Personal Crimes Division. She had the added bonus of being able to work with the diverse populations of the city, endearing herself to any person she managed to win over. Meyers—white, suburban upbringing, privileged—hated that and took great delight in lording his status over Bri. Thinking on it, he was to blame for Max fleeing that night. If only he'd listened, the kid wouldn't be dead and on a slab in Hayes' morgue.

4
LINA

His breath stinks of alcohol when he presses his face into my neck, his hand groping my flesh. I want to pull away, kick him in the balls. I abhor myself for falling for the flowery words and promises of a better life. I haven't seen Max in days, which isn't entirely out of the ordinary. We were moved during the night to a house, shoved inside and told to get ready. Keeping us on the move, I found out, kept the cops from guessing where we were. However, I didn't know if even they could be trusted.

"Spread your legs, bitch. I paid for this." His English is slurred, but polished. I wonder if he is a doctor, a schoolteacher, a lawyer—none of them seem to be below degrading women.

I do as I'm told, no longer able to feel as he forces his way into my body, finishing quickly as I count in my head.

"You're fucking useless." He flips me on my stomach.
1…2…3…4…

Anything would be better than this. Death would be better than this.

5

Bri stared blankly at the computer screen, glancing at the clock indicating it was just past eight in the morning. "This is impossible. Each time we get one of these shit cases, I remember how our city is a haven for all these fuckers looking to exploit women and children."

Peeking around his own monitor, Trent frowned. "Yeah…I know. Makes you feel pretty damned helpless, huh?"

They had been sifting through numerous databases, trying to locate any information about their victim and his sister, Lina. After a twelve-hour shift, Bri knew her routine, however, she was invigorated and angered by this case, more so than she had been by any case in a while. After a quick text to Hayes, Bri knew she would be conducting the autopsy later that day. She had a backlog a mile long, as she covered all types of death not as a result of natural causes, from homicide to accidental.

"Coffee?" Trent stood up and stretched with a groan.

Bri rubbed her eyes. "Yeah, as long as you spring for Starbucks or something. The coffee here tastes like tar. Remember, we have the autopsy at noon."

Making a 'yeah, yeah' motion with his hand, Trent

left. Blinking the gritty feeling from her vision, Bri looked at the screen, jotting down a phone number. Yawning again, she closed her eyes for a brief moment, trying to process everything she had read. If they were going to track down Max and Lina's abductors, they would have to sift through numerous rings and gangs in the city. She wasn't naïve; she knew that every day men, women, and children were brought to the USA under false pretenses. The Triads, the Russian Mafia, even low-level gangsters trafficked in people. It was the easiest way to turn a lengthy profit. Drugs, guns; these were sold once and that was it. A woman could make money for years, and kept under the right 'incentive,' she could hardly object. Objection equaled disposal or serious harm.

"Any update?"

Bri opened her eyes, feeling like only a minute had passed since Trent had left. "Uh, I think we're looking at a Russian organization—weirdly, they tend to stick to their own 'type.'" She shuddered at the word. "Like, for example, the Triads will work in the Asian countries because it's more accessible to them."

"Interesting."

"However, it seems they might have mutual interests...I was reading that Slavic women are considered status symbols in Asian countries, and Asian women are considered exotic by Slavic men. It's all fucking sickening."

"Yeah, I remember being at a conference a year or so ago, and a lot of the women are held under false impressions of debt they owe to their traffickers. It's a low risk endeavor." Trent sat on the edge of Bri's desk, slurping his coffee.

Deciding that further digging into the scum of society would be fruitless without a little sleep behind her, Bri stood and headed to the bunkroom, where officers working on long cases could grab a few hours' sleep.

"Wake me around eleven. Maybe I can get a shower in the locker room before we see Cat."

Trent slumped back into his chair. "Yeah, I'll just kick it here until you're ready."

Smirking, Bri retired to the bunkroom, flopping onto one of the scratchy blankets.

❋ ❋ ❋

"You don't want to think it happens here. No one does. But I guess people live in a bubble." I was sitting with my grandfather in the small living room of their house in the suburbs outside the city.

He studied me as I spoke, his eyes deep pools of brown, kindness and empathy emanating from within, as if I could see into his very soul.

"I feel helpless sometimes. Like I'm not big enough, or strong enough, for this work."

"You bring good to the world, Briana. That is all you need to know. Remember, don't let the burdens of society break you… Your roots run deep. You'll find a way through it to see the good on the other side…"

I watched as he faded, his smile the last to go. I shifted to grasp him, but fell and continued to fall until…

❋ ❋ ❋

Bri jolted awake, her heart pounding against her ribcage. She sat up, nearly banging her head on the metal rungs of the bunk above her. Her mouth was parched, and swallowing became a chore until she stumbled to the bathroom, splashing cool water on her face and shoveling some into her mouth.

Trent's voice called out, muffled by the door. "Hey, you good? We gotta go. Sorry, I kinda fell asleep myself."

Bracing her hands on opposite sides of the sink, Bri stared in the mirror. Her hair was in disarray so she righted it, but nothing could erase the hollow shells of her eyes. "Yeah, coming."

She pushed through the swinging door, almost hitting Trent on the other side.

"Watch it, huh?" He smirked. "Nice bird's nest." He poked at the messy bun on the top of her head. "Trying out for new employment?"

She pushed his arm, even though he easily outweighed her by a hundred pounds. "Shut up. Come on, I'm driving."

"There's a big surprise." He rolled his eyes as he traipsed after her, ever the lost puppy following its master home.

The ride over to the medical examiner's office took place in silence, as these rides often did for the pair. Both knew what they were facing and the fact it was a kid, and one they had had in their precinct, made it that bit more difficult to grasp. Bri watched the traffic as she drove, all the while thinking of the boy.

"I wonder where his sister is…and if she knows her brother is dead."

Trent jolted out of his daydream, processing the statement. "Yeah, tough stuff."

"He told me he didn't have any family—it was just him and Lina."

"I'm still amazed you remember all this."

"Yeah, well, blame my grandfather. He never forgot a thing." She turned into the parking lot, maneuvering into a space.

"I remember meeting him once. He invited me and Christine to a BBQ. Great stories."

Bri remained silent and a panged longing to hear one of her grandfather's stories again caused tears to sting the back of her eyes. "Yeah…let's go see what's up with our vic." It was too raw to think of him as Max, the frightened boy devouring a McDonald's cheeseburger at an alarming rate in front of her.

It was a strange sensation entering the morgue in the

medical examiner's office. No matter how many times she'd been here, Bri always felt an encompassing chill trace through her body. Coupled with the smell of preservatives and a lingering stench of death, it made for quite an unpleasant experience. Trent, on the other hand, didn't seem fazed by anything to do with death. He took it in his stride, Bri noticed. Still, she knew there were some things which would send the six-foot three-inch wall of muscle to his knees.

They were an odd duo, as Bri barely reached his shoulder, but she carried her own power, as beneath her lithe exterior was a set of carefully honed muscles, and the ability to disable a man twice her size with minimal effort. She didn't consider herself a superhero by any means, but the defensive techniques they learned on the force were effective for any person of any size. Regardless of the clear differences in body type, Bri and Trent had each other's backs, and the companionship shared by the pair was envied by many in the department who were left with less than desirable partners.

"Ah, good morning, Inspectors." Dr. Hayes met them at the swinging metal doors leading to the autopsy suite. "You both look like hell."

"Psh, Ryu here might look like hell, but I'm fresh as a daisy." Trent preened dramatically, reducing Bri's tension considerably as she laughed.

Hayes rolled her eyes. "I don't know how you put up with this prima donna." She pushed through the doors, and the feeling Bri had experienced upon entering the building intensified.

"Gloves, please." Hayes gestured to a box, and Bri and Trent followed the usual procedure of snapping on the blue gloves which never fitted quite right.

"We've taken trace samples, but unfortunately, the rain wasn't our friend."

Max's head was propped at an unnatural angle by the

block, his nude body pale and mottled, cleaned and ready for the autopsy. Although she knew she had to remain objective, it always pained Bri to see children on the cold, metal table, their lives cut tragically short by horrible circumstances.

Hayes began efficiently, as she always did. "Male, aged twelve to fourteen. Malnourished…" Max's ribs nearly poked from his flesh. "All teeth removed, along with the tips of his fingers."

"Have you seen anything like that before?"

Hayes lifted her gaze, the bright light reflecting off her glasses. "Yes, once or twice. Usually, if the Mafia—or any crime syndicate for that matter—doesn't want anyone to find a body, they don't. However, I'm just the medical examiner. It's up to you two to figure out the whys and wherefores."

Bri glanced up at Trent. "Maybe a warning of some kind? A don't-fuck-with-us type of thing?"

Trent lifted one of his bulky shoulders, letting it drop. "Dunno. Possible."

Hayes was preparing her instrument tray to begin the internal part of the autopsy. "You guys want to stay for this?"

Bri shook her head. "No, just email me the report ASAP. Oh…his fingertips being removed…post or peri?"

"Post. There are clear indicators of hypostasis—meaning his blood pooled in the lower parts of his body after death, so he was most likely stored on his back, wherever it was. That process takes time, so he was probably killed, and then the body was dealt with about ten hours later. When we got to him, there were no signs of rigor. I'll be able to give a more accurate time of death in my report, but I'd say he was killed over forty-eight hours ago and possibly kept in some sort of refrigeration unit until being…processed, for lack of a better word. There are some signs of thawing, but there's no insect activity that we've found."

Bri tugged at the fingertips of her gloves. "What was his significance, though? If he was just a drug runner, like he said to me six months ago, why would they take this level of care? You'd think they would have just buried him or dumped him in the Bay."

Hayes picked up a scalpel. "Again, hun, not my area of expertise, but I'd be curious to know what you find out." She looked down at the boy's face. "You try not to think too much about these things, but kids…they get me every time."

6

Bri and Trent emerged into the murky afternoon, the sun playing chase behind unpleasant looking clouds.

"You raised some good points. Maybe we need to get an incident room going?"

With a frown, Bri got behind the wheel of the car. "You and I both know the Cap isn't going to want to waste time with a nobody. We have to show him that this is part of a bigger picture. I need to make a few phone calls. We need more information on the situation. It's changing all the time in the city. They're moving more and more women around the Bay Area. I wonder if anyone is tracking this stuff."

"The Feds, most likely, but I have a feeling you don't want to resort to their expertise just yet." Trent fastened his seat belt, fiddling with the radio dial until he found a light rock station. "I suppose we could always pass a hypothetical by them. However, I think we're gonna need to call it for today. Christine's already pissed I didn't come home last night."

As much as Bri hated losing momentum in a case, she knew she'd be much more effective if she did take a few hours to go home, eat something decent, shower, sleep, and change, not necessarily in that order. "Yeah, you're right. Let's head in, give the Cap our initial findings and then reconvene tomorrow."

"Sounds good." Trent leaned heavily on the window. "Shit, I'm beat. Just hit me like a ton of bricks, fucking adrenaline."

Bri understood the crash. It happened to her often enough. It was even more evident as they wearily walked into the captain's office and took seats in front of his desk.

"So, what do we have?" Meyers barely looked up from the sheaf of paperwork he was perusing.

"The victim is a young male, aged twelve to fourteen. I know him from about six months ago as Max, short for Maksym. He and his sister Lina were trafficked into the country from Ukraine." The next part Bri made quite pointed. "He didn't want social work brought in, but you insisted, sir. He fled out the window of the family room and down the fire escape."

Finally, Meyers lifted his gaze with a sharp frown. "I don't remember that."

Trent spoke up, as if he knew Bri would retort in a negative fashion. "Regardless, with Bri's prior knowledge, we can make an ID. I'd like to hold off on releasing an image of him to the media and keep this under wraps until we speak to a few contacts. Last thing we want is the ring holding his sister taking her into hiding, or worse, disposing of her where we won't find her."

Meyers passed his glacial eyes over Bri and focused on Trent, before looking down again. "A good tactic. You might want to try the Anti-Trafficking Coordination Team in Sacramento. They might be able to give you more information about which circles run here in the city. I don't want you to invest too much into this. There's a likelihood we won't ever catch the boy's killer."

Meyers' bluntness had Bri grinding her teeth. She

opened her mouth to speak, but Trent hauled her up by the forearm—a relatively easy task given his strength. "Yes, sir. We'll keep you posted."

As he released her outside the door, Bri spun on him. "What the hell…?"

"Chill, man. I've got your back, but we won't get anything done if you go off the handle at him like that."

She knew he was right, and the anger faded. "You're right. You're always right. You know, you're the only one who can tell me off like that and still live to talk about it."

Trent shot her a boyish grin. "What can I say, I have a gift."

"I don't know how Christine puts up with you."

"Neither do I, Ryu, neither do I."

* * *

BART was delayed, and Bri grumbled as she checked her phone for the time, before glancing around the terminal. A part of her wished Max would pop out from behind one of the concrete pillars and tell her it was a joke. She beat herself up for not doing more at the time. Why hadn't she done more? Why had she brought him into the family room, with a window, knowing he could possibly flee?

Shaking her head, she pushed those negative thoughts to the back of her mind. The greatest justice she could do now for Max was to find Lina and get her away from the traffickers, but even Bri knew that was a next to impossible task. Still, she owed it to Max to try. His sunken blue eyes reflected back to her in the dark corners of the underground station. She made a silent promise that she would do all she could, even if it meant ruffling some feathers.

And what about the other girls? Even though the city only had about sixty homicides a year, Bri had seen her fair share of female victims, some murdered in domestic violence conflicts, some never to be identified. And then there were the missing women. It was too much to process. She recalled her dad's mantra: "Leave your work at work," but sometimes, it was simply impossible. Her relationships over the years had greatly suffered from her work baggage. It seemed only other people who worked in the profession truly got it.

The BART train screeched to a stop, sending a high-pitched noise echoing through the terminal. Bri winced, as she did every time. It was reflexive. Stepping aside to allow the outflow of passengers to descend from the train, she then boarded, finding a spot by the window, and plugged in her headphones. The elegant tones of Lindsey Stirling filled her head, the emotional instrumental music chasing away the cobwebs. While Trent preferred his oldies, Bri needed something without the distraction of lyrics at that moment. Glancing down at her iPhone, she marked the title of the song, "Lost Girls." Nothing could be more fitting. The frantic notes reflected her thoughts perfectly. How many lost girls were there in the city?

She peered around the carriage, noticing that it was relatively quiet for the time of day. In one corner a teenager had his hood up and his head was bobbing to the music probably blasting out his ears. Two older women sat, shopping bags between them, carrying on a loud conversation, shouting to be heard over the obnoxiously loud squeals of metal wheels on track. Aside from that, there were no other signs of activity.

It was coming on three in the afternoon when Bri arrived in South City. Luckily, the one-bedroom apartment she rented was right across from the station, so she didn't have far to walk. It made owning a car pointless, really, since she spent most of her time at home or work, but she still had one—a newish Ford Focus which occupied her assigned parking space at the complex.

Opening the door to the cool, dark apartment, Bri realized how little time she spent here. Her carpets were spotless and furniture still nearly new. It looked like a show home, set up for potential renters rather than a lived-in domicile. She looked at the blinking number on her answering machine and hit 'delete.' If anyone wanted to contact her, they knew her cell phone was the best way, and even then, it was sketchy if they'd get in contact with her or not.

Tossing her messenger bag onto the couch, she walked to the fridge, opening it and staring at the bare interior. "Chinese food it is," she muttered, slamming it shut and fiddling through a stack of menus on the counter.

After the voice on the phone told her it would be forty-five minutes, she decided a shower was in order. If there was one thing Bri loved about this place, it was the shower—hot with a steady, strong pressure to work out all the lingering kinks in her back and shoulders. As she leaned against the tiled wall, eyes closed, her thoughts drifted back to an earlier time, one where she was under the impression she could balance a job like this and a family. A lot of cops did it, working long hours and then going home to the wife and two-point-five kids. She'd tried, she really had, but it just wasn't in the cards.

Her ex-girlfriend, Sarah, had given it her best, she really had…at first. Then the fights started about the late nights, the lack of desire to go out, even just for dinner. When Bri got home, the last thing she wanted to do was fight the crowds, her eyes always looking for suspicious behavior. It came with the territory, and Sarah just couldn't get her head around it. Finally, one night when Bri had come home after a twelve-hour shift, Sarah had been waiting at the table. She'd told her she had met someone else. Bri's temper had risen and then fizzled out.

She couldn't blame Sarah and had wished her well. Still, it would have been nice, sometimes, to come home and have someone special waiting with open arms and an understanding smile, someone who had no expectations and understood the job, but that had yet to happen.

Bri pushed down the handle controlling the water on the shower and it shut off. She wrapped a giant towel around her body and used another to roughly dry her shoulder-length hair before wrapping it in a toweling turban. She was just pulling on a tank top when the doorbell dinged. Finally, her head began to calm as she ate beef chow mein and pot stickers in front of Netflix.

7
LINA

The girl in the corner of the room is crying again, and most of the other girls know why. No one cries like that unless they have reason anymore. Condoms are supplied to us more than food—a pregnant whore is no use. I heard her tell another girl that she thought the man would pay more, so she stopped using them. Silly fool. Doesn't she know our debts will just be compounded, pushed to an astronomical amount we can no longer even dream of paying off?

Fleetingly, my mind skips to Max. What has happened to him? He would come religiously, every Saturday. It was the small mercy they allowed him if he met his quota. Maybe he hadn't done that…but it must have been…two weeks now since I last saw him. I hope he is alright.

Escapism is all I have left. I had wanted to be an actress. Leon promised there were many opportunities for this in America. As I lie on my narrow bed, I cannot even feel pain. When Leon met me in Ukraine, one of the first things he did was take me to the movies. We saw *Alice Through the Looking Glass* with Johnny Depp. I loved

Johnny Depp. When Alice fell through the mirror and landed in Wonderland, I smiled. I was like Alice. I liked to believe in the impossibilities—dreams I thought I'd never achieve, but maybe with Leon by my side, I could.

Only, I didn't fall into Wonderland.

I fell into hell.

8

The alarm on her phone blared to life in a series of annoying musical tones. Bri rolled over, jabbing her finger blindly at the screen until it ceased. Bleary-eyed, she fumbled into the kitchen and filled the kettle, shoving it onto the stove top and turning the dial. Her mom had said she should get one of those Tassimo things, but the thought of all the wasted pods had her cringing. Good ol' water and tea bags were fine. Besides, she could chuck the tea bags in the compost bin out behind the complex.

Shuddering as a huge yawn racked her body, she leaned on the counter, waiting for the water to boil. As she did, her phone rang. It was Trent. She answered with a grunt, pulling the phone away so he couldn't hear her second, ear-splitting yawn—Bri was not a morning person.

"Morning yourself. Sleep well?"

The water began to rumble. "Like the princess and the pea."

"Huh?"

Bri shook her head. "Never mind. What couldn't wait until I got there?"

"Autopsy report."

Reaching up into the cupboard, she plunked a mug on the counter, adding a tea bag and a spoonful of sugar. "Anything Hayes didn't already predict?"

"Just the cause of death."

Bri's hand jolted, and granules of sugar sprinkled the counter. "Shit," she muttered, abruptly awakened by the thought of new knowledge surrounding the case.

"What?"

"Just spilled sugar. Go on."

"Drug overdose."

The kettle whistled, and Bri removed it from the heat. "Interesting. Which?"

"Heroin. Strange thing is, there's no indication he was a user."

Her phone beeped, and she pulled it back as a text from her mom dropped down from the top of the screen. Ignoring it, she put the phone on the counter and hit the speaker button. "Right, so, they give him a lethal dose of drugs and then process the body like a mob hit? It's conflicting practices."

"I know. It's like they wanted us to assume he was a druggie, but the fingertips and teeth indicate he had some importance." Trent's voice echoed off the linoleum and tile in her kitchen.

"Unless he knew something…or had found out something he wasn't supposed to." She bobbed the teabag in and out of the hot water, watching brown swirl into the cup.

"Yeah, maybe. We need to call ICE today and see if there's anything on him…maybe they have a photograph database?"

"You think they'll let us run Max's image through it?"

"Either that, or they'll do it for us, but fuck knows how long that'll take…" There were the muted sounds of a female's voice in the background. "Look, I'll catch you later at the precinct."

"Yeah...take care." Bri heard the familiar triple beep of him ending the call, and she stared at her cell, musing to herself. "What were you up to, Max? Why were you so afraid?"

Sighing, she squeezed the water out of the teabag with the back of a spoon and gave the tea a stir before taking it to the couch. She didn't usually have much time in the mornings, but this was a small ritual she enjoyed. It gave her time to reflect more on the case and mentally prepare herself for the day ahead, or evening, depending on her shifts. She ran off a checklist of the things still to do, including get a hold of the ATC Team to see if they had any information on circles running in the city, and read the autopsy report on Max. Then, hopefully, armed with that, they could get out and start questioning people.

*　*　*

"Here. You look starved." Trent pushed an old-fashioned chocolate donut on a napkin across their joined desks.

"Thanks." After her tea, Bri had wanted nothing more than to get to work as fast as she could. As per usual, she had forgotten to eat, but Trent was prepared. As she meticulously broke off the edges of the donut, popping each piece into her mouth, she skimmed the autopsy report.

Trent came around and leaned over her shoulder. "Whatcha think?"

"I think the kid never had a chance." She pointed to the monitor. "Look. Hayes says there was no indication of anything in his stomach. He had bruising to his arms and abdomen, and abrasions to his back and legs. No track marks on his arms or between his toes, just the single injection mark in the crook of his elbow."

"She said she would send his blood samples to tox to get a definite answer on the amount given to him."

Bri looked up to Trent. "Given?"

"Yeah...I'm under the impression, based on what you've said, that the kid wouldn't have done this to himself. He wanted to save his sister, right? How could he do that if he was dead?"

"True enough." Bri dusted the crumbs off her hand. "Right, so, should I call Sac, or will you?"

"Not it." Trent laughed and slumped back into his chair.

"Asshole. You know I don't like talking to the Feds."

"Shoulda called it faster."

Bri shot him a menacing glare and picked up the phone. The receptionist on the other end sounded bored, putting Bri on hold for what seemed like an indeterminable amount of time. When it felt like she'd rolled her eyes for the hundredth time at Trent, a deep, rich voice filled her ear.

"This is Special Agent Kastner."

"Hello, this is Inspector Briana Ryu at SFPD. We were looking for information regarding a homicide case we're working at the moment. We believe the victim was trafficked to San Francisco from Ukraine and that his sister may still be alive and..."

"Hold on."

Bri raised her eyebrows, giving Trent a perplexed shrug. He mouthed the word, "What?" and she shook her head as Kastner's voice came back on the line.

"Name?"

"I don't have a last name, but his first name is Maksym, goes by Max. He came to us about six months ago..."

"Email me a photograph. I'll see what I can do."

Bri felt her temper rising. "Look here. I don't care that you're a Fed, and you have to lower yourself to help a local police force, but this kid came to me about six months ago and something had scared him shitless. So lose the attitude, *Agent* Kastner. We're all looking to the same goal here."

Silence. For a brief moment, Bri thought he'd hung up on her.

"My apologies, Inspector Ryu. You must understand that we get these calls all the time and there's usually very little we can do in the way of tracing these victims."

"That's all you had to say in the first place, but I'd appreciate any help you can provide." Bri managed to soothe back her anger, but her teeth remained gritted.

"Sorry for being curt. Email me what you have, and I'll get back to you ASAP." He rattled off a Federal email address, and Bri jotted it down.

"Thanks."

Trent's eyes widened expectantly as he waited for the rundown.

"I doubt they'll be much help. He seemed like I was imposing on him more than anything." She stared at the picture of Max's lifeless face on her monitor. "We might have to handle the legwork ourselves."

"I did find a few charities in the city that work with trafficking victims. Maybe one of them can be helpful? Like, if we show Max's picture around, someone might recognize him?"

"It's worth a shot."

"There's a phone number here for a woman who runs one of the shelters." Trent tapped on his keyboard. "It's called Haven." He reached over for the phone.

Bri zoned out as he made the call, thinking of what Max's sister must be going through. He might have been beaten and starved, but her fate was going to be much worse. Max had seemed to be a smart kid, so what had drawn his sister to bring him to the USA? The tactics used by these so-called recruiters were perfected over years of practice. The men, and occasionally women, knew how to play to a victim's insecurities. So, what had this one promised Lina to make her uproot her brother?

Trent waved his hand in front of her face. "Earth to Bri, come in, Bri."

She batted his hand away. "What?"

He grinned. "Got through to Haven. We're going to meet the woman in an hour at a Starbucks. The location of the actual shelter is confidential, for obvious reasons."

"Uh huh…"

"Where'd your mind go just now?" He linked his fingers behind his head, leaning back in his chair and swaying side to side.

Bri grumbled, hating it when he tried to unpick her thought process on a case, but knowing that bouncing her ideas off him was often the best way to do it. "I was thinking about what lured Max's sister to want to come to the USA in the first place. They both sounded like intelligent kids."

"Some of those guys are master manipulators." He lowered his voice. "It's like with you and Hank…you knew it was wrong, but you still made excuses…"

Scowling, Bri crossed her arms. "I hate when you're right."

"Naw, you just hate being reminded of your perceived failings." Trent smirked. "Hey, it was just an example."

Hank was an ex-boyfriend, who had decided that verbally berating Bri was the best way to get her to quit her job and fall into the wife and mother role he wanted. He came from money, his parents both highly paid and respected attorneys. Where he'd gotten it into his head that women should stay at home, Bri had no idea. She surmised later that it must have stemmed from his own mother not being home a lot while he was growing up. However, Hank had gone about getting this across in the entirely wrong way. Eventually, Bri had told him to get the hell out, and after a string of degrading names, he finally had left. She'd heard he'd gone on to marry some Barbie doll wannabe, had two kids, and they were living in

Menlo Park.

"It's a pretty sad state of affairs when I can't find a good man or woman in this city, Billy."

"Eh, it's not so bad." He lifted his arms above his head in a stretch and then cracked his neck. "Think we should hit the gym after this? You're lookin' a bit chubby. Must be all the donuts."

Bri stuck out her tongue, knowing he was trying to draw her from her funk. "Blame my enabling partner. Yeah, that sounds good. Exercise'll clear these cobwebs from my brain. Well, if we have an hour to kill, I'll update our case file. By the way, I think we should pull footage from the security tapes of when Max was here. I never looked at them after he bolted that first time."

Trent spun a final time in his chair. "On it." He sauntered off toward the IT department, hands tucked in his pockets.

Shaking her head with a smile, Bri commenced her most hated task—paperwork.

* * *

An hour passed quickly, and Trent hadn't returned from IT. Muttering to herself, Bri went in search of her wayward partner and found him with Kevin Freedman, their computer specialist, heads together staring at a screen.

"What's going on?"

The men, startled, collided with a thunk, resembling the sound of coconuts hitting together. They rubbed their respective heads, moaning.

"Seriously, I didn't think it took this long to pass on a message about video footage."

Trent straightened. "Has it been an hour? Shit, sorry. We got sidetracked trying to clear up the tape from the front of the building, when you came in with Max. There's someone who followed, stopped at the door, and then retreated. Freeze it, Kev."

Freedman, who had recovered much more quickly from his bump, tapped a few keys. He was probably just shy of twenty-five and a whiz at technology. His attempts to look his age this week had culminated in a scruffy attempt at a goatee which someone would eventually say made him look like a hipster, and he'd shave it off for the next day.

"Look here, see? It's kinda shadowy, but it's there." He poked the monitor gently, not willing to damage his prize equipment.

Bri squinted. "Can you enhance it?"

"Nope, too dark, but yeah. He's there. He sticks around for about twenty minutes…" Freedman advanced the time. "…and he leaves here."

Bri met Trent's eyes over the top of Freedman's head. "You think maybe it wasn't the Cap who startled him, but he somehow knew this guy was there?"

"Anything is possible."

"Mark it and add it to our files, will ya, Kev?"

"No probs, Inspector."

Motioning to the door, she led Trent out. "We'll have to explore this when we get back. I have a feeling your contact won't take kindly to us being late."

9
LINA

The crying girl is gone. I imagine they took her either early this morning or sometime in the night. They have an older Russian woman looking after us. She is not kind, and her face resembles that of a nun who used to teach us back home, one who used to hit our hands with rulers if we did not answer correctly or in time. Before our parents died, things were good. Max and I had plenty of food and clothing. Then the accident happened, and I had to drop out of school. I had wanted to go to university, study acting. Instead, I worked in a dingy café, serving cheap food to university students.

I remember the day Leon came to the café. He was handsome, too handsome to notice someone as ordinary as I was, but he sat at a table near the counter, flashing me a perfectly straight white smile. Color burned in my cheeks as I served him a coffee and one of the fresh baked pastries. He took my wrist gently, asking me if I'd like to have dinner with him.

I wish I'd said no.

10

They opted to walk to the meeting, rather than face the uncertainties of parking, especially since it was going on five and the evening commute would start soon, cramming the streets with cars. The sun was descending below the tall buildings, and a chilly breeze originating from the Bay weaved its way through the people, cutting through jackets and jeans. Bri hugged her arms around her body, while Trent strolled along like the cold air was nothing.

"It's not fair."

"What?" He glanced over at her.

"You don't ever get cold."

In a joking gesture, he wrapped one of his arms around her. "'Cause you've got nothing to you, Ryu."

She shoved him off. "Hey, hey, now, we're on duty."

"Psh." He turned the corner. "Here it is."

They ducked through the door of the busy coffee shop. Trent looked around, his height affording him that advantage. "At the back." Weaving their way between businesspeople on laptops and teenagers on cell phones, they finally reached a table where a slim woman, with caramel-colored skin and jet-black hair pulled back in a neat ponytail, sat. Her eyes were wide and a brilliant shade of hazel, but there was an old soul behind the youthful face, someone who had seen the worst in society.

"Hi, I'm Inspector Billy Trent. We spoke on the phone?" Trent took the lead, which Bri was all too happy to allow him to do.

"Hello again, Inspector." She smiled up from the large espresso mug, her eyes passing over Bri.

"This is my partner, Inspector Briana Ryu. This is Petra Vasquez."

The women shook hands before Bri sat opposite Petra. Trent made a 'coffee' gesture, and Bri nodded. As he went to wait in the line, Bri shuffled out of her jacket, placing it on the back of the chair.

"When your partner called, he said you were looking for information about a boy. We only work with women in our shelters, so I do not know if I can be of help." There was a light, musical accent to her speech.

"Well, we have reason to believe his sister may still be in danger."

"It is unusual for the girls to come with male siblings. I would be curious to know why the exception was made. Saying that, if a girl seems that she will be of particularly high value, they are willing to appease her in any way possible."

Bri folded her hands. "If I can be honest, I'm at a loose end with this one. I know our captain will pull the plug if we don't show progress and the investigation will be relegated to the cold case department. I don't want that to happen. Max deserves better."

Petra smiled, and Bri's attention was drawn to her full lips. She mentally admonished herself— this was no time to be considering any kind of romantic thoughts. "I see. How did you meet the boy?"

Trent returned with coffee, setting a white mug in front of Bri.

"In a BART station. He came up to me and asked for help for him and his sister, who had been brought here from Ukraine. I brought him back to the station, and before I could ask him more, he fled. We…didn't follow it up because well, what could we do? Then, two days ago, he turned up in an alley, murdered. Initially we thought it was because he overheard me and the captain discussing social work, but today we found footage that someone followed us to the precinct."

None of the details seemed to shake Petra, who methodically sipped her coffee. "In truth, there is often very little we can do. These traffickers move the women around so much, some of them don't even know what city they are in."

"How is that possible?" Trent piped up. "It's not like we're in small town America."

"They keep them away from windows, drug them, move them around a lot… One girl thought she was in London. You have to understand, Inspector, these people don't want the girls to have any hope. Hence why I say it is unusual to see a brother and a sister trafficked together to the same city."

"Her name is Lina…"

"There are many Linas, Inspector Ryu, unfortunately. It is a common name in the Slavic countries."

Bri withdrew the picture of Max. "I know it's probably futile, but do you recognize him?"

Their hands brushed as Petra took the photograph, studying it carefully in the low lighting. "He…does not look familiar to me, but…" She heaved a sigh. "I do not like to do this because the girls in our care have been through extensive trauma and abuse…"

"Please. I mean, it sounds silly, but I guess I'd like to maybe at least try to get to Lina. It's a shot in the dark, yeah, but I owe it to Max." Bri knew the revelation wouldn't come as a shock to Trent. He knew how passionately she took certain cases, especially those involving kids.

"I will show it to the girls. Give me a few days, please. Then we can meet here again?"

Relief poured from Bri. "Thank you, so much."

Finishing their respective coffees, the trio stood. Petra was about equal height with Bri. "You know, Inspector, perhaps you are in the wrong profession? In my experience, law enforcement does not often allow people to do the most good." She smiled to both and departed.

Bri gaped after the woman until Trent nudged her shoulder.

"I've seen that look before. Like a teenager with a crush."

Shoving him back harder, she growled, "Shut up."

* * *

"Tox is back on the vic." Trent handed Bri the folder sitting on the top of his inbox when they got back to the office.

Skimming the numbers, Bri sighed. "Heroin in a high concentration was found in his system, more than enough to kill a healthy man, let alone a child."

Trent glanced over his shoulder at the open door of Captain Meyers' office. "Should we…?" He jerked his head.

Bri set the paper down with a labored exhale. "Yeah…guess we have to keep him up to date."

The pair reluctantly made their way toward the door to the office. "Cap? We have COD."

Meyers looked up from his computer. "Right. What is it?" He motioned them in, and Trent shut the door.

"Heroin overdose, it seems like."

"So, the kid ODed, and the people he worked for didn't want us tracing them, so they dumped the body?"

"I don't think it's that simple, sir." Bri stepped

forward. "We've seen the video from the night he came here, remember?" She wanted to drive the point home that if not for Meyers, they might have been able to do something rather than scrambling for tenuous connections now, but she knew that might not have been the case.

"Yes…" Meyers' eyes darkened.

"I think someone followed him here."

Running a hand through his salt and pepper hair, Meyers shifted his gaze between the two of them. "You want to dedicate more time to this, even if it means hours of police work and potentially coming up dry?"

"We have calls in to the FBI taskforce up in Sac, and we've been speaking to a woman who runs a shelter for women who have been trafficked."

Bri was glad Trent was the one to mention the FBI. It would be better coming from him than her. Still, Meyers would know who had made the initial suggestion. This was made obvious by the way his eyes bored into her as soon as Trent mentioned the Feds.

"I see. Well, seeing as you've already made some headway, stick with it, but I want daily updates, and if something else comes along that I need you to work on, you leave this case to the side, got it?"

"Yes, sir," they piped up in unison.

Upon exiting the office, Bri let out the breath she had been holding and slumped against the wall.

Trent clapped a hand onto her shoulder. "I know. We all have those cases…the ones we can't drop. Hell, at least he's letting us investigate."

Bri knew Trent still carried the burden of the case of a missing girl in the East Bay, when he worked for Oakland PD. He still scanned the Jane Doe lists every time they entered the coroner's office.

"Yeah, but how far are we gonna get?" The strings holding together their case so far were all based on circumstantial evidence. Until they found something concrete, there wasn't much they could do.

Trent smiled with casual optimism. "Just gotta wait and see."

Waiting and seeing was not something Bri did well.

//

With nothing else better to do, going home seemed like the only viable option for Bri. Again, she found herself looking over her shoulder in the BART terminal, before shaking her head at the sheer stupidity of it. For the entire ride, she stared off into space, fiddling with the feathery end of her braid, flicking it back and forth over her fingers. She willed things to move faster, knowing these first hours of the investigation were crucial, but it frustrated her that things were moving at a snail's pace.

The sky was dingy gray as she walked from the station, and as she rounded the corner, she felt the first heavy drops of rain. By the time she reached her apartment, the clouds had opened into a steady, cold downpour, soaking her to the skin. Her hands shook as she opened the apartment door and she quickly stripped off her soaking wet clothing, replacing it with warm sweatpants and a T-shirt. As she tugged the cotton material over her head, her cell phone rang.

"Hello?"

"Bri! You're a hard one to catch."

"Oh, hi, Mom." She fell onto the couch. "What's new?"

"Just the lack of communication from my eldest daughter."

"Uh, been busy. Caught a case, so things have been rushed."

"Are you still coming this weekend? Your brother is bringing his new girlfriend to meet the family."

Her brother, Nate, seemed to have a new girl every week. "How long is this one gonna last?"

"He seems really happy with her. Your sister is coming as well…with the kids."

Bri inwardly groaned. Her niece and nephew were two of the most spoiled children in the Bay Area. Granted, she knew it wasn't their fault—their parents indulged them out of guilt for working long hours to provide for the family. It was the burden of families in the high-priced area. You worked to live. She had decided a long time ago that she wouldn't have children, and when she'd made this revelation to her mother, it had resulted in a week-long silent treatment, even after Bri had reminded her that she had two other children perfectly capable of providing her with grandchildren to spoil.

"Right. It's still on Saturday?"

"Goodness, Briana, you'd think you could remember a family get together. Yes, Saturday. Tomorrow. Maybe you could bring that partner of yours. He's nice."

Her mother couldn't get it through her head that Trent was a friend and coworker, not a potential husband. Even so, Bri could never think of him like that. She'd seen too many work relationships complicated by sexual impulses.

"No, Ma, remember? He has a girlfriend…"

"Oh, right. Anyway, I have to go. Your father wants to go to the store. Bye!"

Click. Bri stared blankly at the screen, before tossing her cell aside. Maybe she could go along, then pretend to get a call and escape. Maybe she could coerce Trent into the scheme. She leaned back into the couch cushions and closed her eyes, unable to shake the feeling that there was more to Max's death than just the disposal of a boy who knew too much. Reaching for her phone again, she texted Hayes.

Hey, anything unusual on our vic?

The reply came almost instantly. *Nothing I can see. Trace is still working.*

Absolutely nothing in the stomach? Anything to trace his whereabouts?

I'll look again in the morning just for you. What you up to?

Laying here, feeling sorry for myself.

I'll be over in ten.

Bri jolted to a seated position. Her fingers hovered over the screen. Did she want company? It would help take her mind off the case, but she knew she'd end up talking shop with Hayes. Sighing, she typed in a single letter: *K*.

* * *

Minimal effort was made on Bri's part to do anything with her appearance for Hayes' unexpected visit; meaning, she didn't even change. However, she did take the liberty of ordering pizza, the standard fare to go with the imported beer she knew Hayes would bring. It was like everyone around her had a sixth sense—they knew when she was stewing about a case. If it wasn't Hayes, it'd be Trent. *Maybe they have a rotation schedule worked out.* She chuckled at the thought.

Becoming friends with Hayes had been a complete fluke. They had just clicked upon meeting for the first time, after a homeless man had been found strangled in Golden Gate Park. Hayes had asked if Bri wanted to grab a drink—in a strictly platonic sense—after the autopsy. These sorts of things were standard in Bri's world but would have probably appeared very strange to someone not involved in law enforcement. It was how you coped with all the crap around you—pretend things were normal for the sake of keeping your sanity.

She'd found out that Hayes was also born and bred in the Bay Area, the second generation of a family of Mexican immigrants. She'd married young, a white man who her family didn't approve of, but got divorced soon after, keeping his last name. Bri had never asked why, assuming it was a personal matter. She'd put herself through medical school, then completed her fellowship in Forensic Pathology. It had taken her a bit of bouncing around, but she'd eventually come to rest in San Francisco, where she had the cleanest track record of anyone Bri had met.

The doorbell rang, and Bri wandered over, wine glass in hand. "Hey."

Hayes eyed her up and down. "I can see you dressed for the occasion."

"Yeah, well, what can I say? I wasn't expecting anyone." Their banter was lighthearted, and Bri tugged her friend into the apartment.

"Yeesh, you really should get some color in here. It's blinding me."

"Psh, you say that every time." Bri moved into the living room. "Vino or beer?"

Hayes held up the non-descript brown bag. "Beer, as always."

Taking the bag, Bri meandered toward the kitchen. "Glass or can?"

"What am I, a rich bitch? Can, of course."

Bri removed the beer from the bag and put it into the fridge, grabbing a bottle of wine and a glass and bringing a can into the living room, where Hayes had already made herself at home, shoes off, feet tucked under her. "Thanks." She popped the tab and took a long drink. "Ah, hits the spot."

Flopping down next to her, Bri tossed Hayes the remote. "You pick."

"Oooo, there's a new series of *Outlander* on Prime." She fiddled with the buttons.

Bri groaned. "No, not the Scottish thing. Please! What did I do to you in a past life to be subjected to such torture?" She gagged dramatically.

Hayes shoved her arm. "Shut up. He's so hot."

"Ugh." Bri pouted but still couldn't help smiling. For a fleeting moment, she felt at ease.

After two episodes of Hayes swooning and the consumption of pizza, both sat in a lull of silence as the previous episode began to cycle to the next.

"It's just I feel guilty…" This happened every time they hung out. Laughter, some cheesy period drama, and Bri using Hayes as a counsellor to come to terms with whichever case was eating at her.

"I knew you would be. This is the same kid who caught you at the BART station a few months back?"

Bri nodded. "Yeah…I shouldn't have left the room…"

"I can't begin to speculate on the motives people have when they do things, but this boy…what's happened to him…isn't your fault, Bri. There's a shit-ton of bad people out there, and when you get a large population concentrated in one place, you're going to have people doing a lot of fucked up things."

"Yeah, I know, it's just the more and more I read about these traffickers, the more and more I realize what I don't know."

"But this isn't your area of expertise, Bri. The problem is pervasive in the city, no question, however, you can't save everyone."

"I just wish I could shake this feeling it all runs deeper. That there's going to be a happy ending here."

"It's not like the movies. Sometimes, real life doesn't

end happily. You yourself should know that."

Bri opened the bottle of red wine and poured herself a glass. "Yes, but I don't need to be reminded of it." The rim had just touched her lips when her cell rang. "Shit." She checked the screen, shooting Hayes a concerned look. "It's Trent."

"Hey, Bri, sorry to interrupt your evening, but I need you and Hayes to come back in."

"How'd you…?"

"Intuition. Come on."

"Wait, what's up?"

"We have another body."

12
LINA

They tell us that the crying girl is not coming back, and we should do well to listen to instructions from now on. I learned from one who sleeps near me that her name is…was Ariadne. I have made no assumptions about her fate. Those of us who do not conform to what is required end up beaten, raped, or dead. I wonder, though, why they did not just remove the baby and send her back here. That's what happened before, to other girls.

There are whispers coming from the hallway. They have left the door cracked for some reason—I no longer question their motivations.

"She went mad." I recognize the voice of the big woman who watches over us and makes sure we are free from diseases, and that the bruises are hidden. We are less valuable infected or damaged.

"You make sure those girls use the condoms until we can get birth control."

"She fought. She did not want us to remove the baby. In the end, she bled too much. You must find a better doctor for these things."

A grunt and heavy footsteps retreat down the hall. The door flies open, and I yank the thin blanket over my head, pretending to sleep. I can hear her footsteps now, lighter, but slow, as if trying to catch someone out. When she finds no disobedience, she departs, shutting the door softly.

I want to weep. Punished for something she had no control over, such is the way of these men. I think of Max. Maybe they see I am so afraid, they have no more need of him. He was my last hope, even if I didn't want him to get help for us. How could he, really? Maybe he knew where we are being kept...I certainly don't.

I blame myself for our circumstances. Surely I should have known better than to trust Leon. After our first date, he had asked to come back to our home, showing shock at the living conditions, the lack of food. I did my best to keep things clean, but I was struggling. Max was a growing boy, and I did not want him to have to quit school, like I had had to do. I wanted him to go on to get a good job.

I remember hanging my head in shame, but Leon touched my cheek and kissed me. My heart leapt at his affection. He did not try more and promised he would bring us nice food the next day. With that, he left. I dared to hope, but I wondered if he would not fulfill his promise. However, I was proved wrong when he arrived the next day with two bags full of food. I was overjoyed, kissing him repeatedly. Still, he took it no further and sat while I prepared the three of us a meal. We ate until we thought we would burst.

That night, he spoke to both of us of America...of the good schools Max could attend...of the acting and singing jobs I could get. After a while, even the doubt in Max's eyes began to fade as we both imagined such a life.

What do they call it...rose-colored glasses? By the end of the night, he'd had them firmly attached to our faces.

13

Flood lights illuminated the bank of the Islais Creek in Glen Canyon Park. Trent stood off to the side as Bri and Hayes approached, having taken Bri's car. Both flashed ID to the officer at the edge of the yellow crime scene tape. Hayes split off, going to change into her protective gear, taking over from the other medical examiner. Bri slogged through the soft ground over to Trent's side.

"What's up?"

"Female, young, found by a couple of teenagers looking for a quiet spot to have some alone time. I sent them home in a squad car. They said they saw her and called 911 immediately, so there's not much else to ask. Guess they'd seen a couple episodes of *CSI* 'cause they didn't disturb the scene."

Bri nodded, squinting over to Hayes kneeling by the side of a pale human form. "Let's let the techs do their job. Shit...this'll be the excuse Meyers needs to take us off Max's case..."

"Don't jump to conclusions yet. We might be able to pass this one off to another team..."

"I don't think either of you want to do that." Hayes walked toward them, her protective suit rustling. "She's been given the same treatment as your other victim."

Watching as the techs zipped the body into a black bag, Bri shook her head. "What the hell is going on?"

"It's not up to me to speculate, Inspectors, but I think you've got someone trying to warn you—or maybe someone else—to stay out of their territory."

"Territory?" Trent's eyebrow shot up curiously.

"Look, the last time I saw such a strategic placement of bodies in the open, there was a turf war going on between gang members in the East Bay. The sooner you hear back from the Feds and your contact, the better."

"Wait, how did you know…"

"There was one poking around the coroner's office. Guy in a suit, looked decidedly grumpy according to one of my techs. He told them to talk to you two. Speaking of which…" Hayes jerked her head to the approaching headlights. "Looks like he's caught wind of our latest find."

A man in a wrinkled black suit made his way through the grass toward them. "Special Agent Robert Kastner. We spoke on the phone?" He skimmed his gaze over Bri, and she balked at his probative stare.

"Yeah, we did. How can we help you?" She crossed her arms, fixing him with hard glare.

"I'm here about your victim…victims, so it seems." He craned his neck, trying to see past her to the body being loaded into the van. "We'll need to take jurisdiction."

"Pardon me? Have you talked to Captain Meyers?" Trent stepped alongside Bri.

"We don't need to."

"Look, Agent Kastner, we called you asking for help and you said you'd 'look into it.' Now, here you are, at *our* crime scene, so if you want us to cooperate, you'd better start talking." Bri strummed her fingers on her upper arm. She was taking no prisoners. This was her case, and she was damned if she was going to hand it over to the Feds without a good reason.

Kastner stepped forward, and Bri marked his intense blue eyes and mussed blond hair. He was her age, maybe a few years older; it was hard to tell as this job often made people look older than their years. "I appreciate your work so far, Inspector Ryu, but this is beyond your scope of understanding, and you'll just end up getting in the way."

"Damned if you know that!" Her response came out a bit more forced than she'd planned, and Trent placed a hand on her shoulder. She shook him off, squaring up to the cocky Fed. "Our turf, our rules. We work together or I call my Cap right now and he calls the commissioner, who I don't think will take kindly to Feds showing up without warning."

Kastner must have been rattling through the ramifications of an uninvited investigation takeover by the FBI because he cast his eyes skyward momentarily, before fixing them back on Bri. "If you mess this up…"

"I'll take the blame." Her tone softened. "I just want to know what is going on in my city. I don't think that's too much to ask. If we leave it up to you guys, we'll never know what happened to Max or his sister…"

"Lina."

Bri blinked several times. "Yes, Lina. How the hell…?"

Kastner reached into the inside pocket of his suit jacket, withdrawing a piece of paper. "Maksym and Melina Pavlok. Arrived in the United States via San Francisco International Airport from Ukraine approximately a year ago on visitor visas. Both expired six months ago, but there has been no sign of them since, according to ICE. They were sponsored by a man named Leon Skiliar, a name we learned was fake. Not unusual—people disappear into this country every day. But if they were trafficked, you have to understand, Inspectors, these criminal rings are very sophisticated, and they work at not being caught."

"We've been discussing the prospect of a trafficking ring operating in the city, Agent Kastner." Trent, clearly having seen the state of shock on Bri's face, continued the conversation.

"Trafficking rings are everywhere, but yes, I would say this is a highly organized one, possibly connected to the Russian mafia, judging on the ethnicity of their victims."

"That backs up what Max told me about him and his sister coming from Ukraine." Bri found her tongue finally.

"The trouble is, as you've no doubt found in your own research, we have trouble tracking them. These operations are mobile, never staying in one place for long."

The van containing the body of the young woman drove off into the night. Bri looked after it with a measured exhale of breath. "I would really like to work together on this, Agent Kastner. Do you think we could collaborate?"

As each flood light was removed, eerie shadows cast themselves across the agent's face. Mentally, Bri crossed her fingers, hoping he would agree. She still felt a duty to Max.

"I'd like to talk to your captain. If he gives the approval, I'll take it to my supervisor." With that, Kastner returned to his car and drove off, leaving Bri and Trent in near darkness at the side of the creek.

"Funny dude," Trent remarked, tucking his hands into his pockets.

Bri twisted her hair around her finger, twirling it into a half-hearted bun before letting it unfurl back into a ponytail. "Yeah…really uptight. Still, he's giving us a good chance to find Max's sister with his connections. I say, we roll with it."

"Roll with it?" Trent pressed a hand to her forehead. "You feelin' all right?"

She slapped at his hand. "Hey!"

Trent laughed. "Give me a ride back to the station?"

"I suppose." The thought fleetingly crossed her mind that this could be Lina.

"What, no witty retort?"

Bri shook her head, glancing back at the fluttering crime scene tape. "Not tonight."

14

On the way back to the station, Bri took a detour, pulling up at the medical examiner's office. Trent shifted in the passenger seat. "What are we doing here? Hayes won't have the autopsy results for at least another twenty-four hours."

"We didn't get to see the body very clearly." Bri knew it was an excuse. She was anxious to start making headway. With this being the second body so close to the other, something more had to be going on.

Stepping out of the car, she spotted Kastner's car. "What's he doing here?" she mumbled.

Trent swiveled. "Oh…it's the Fed."

Bri nearly ran into the office, with Trent on her heels. When they reached reception, she saw Hayes, head bent, deep in conversation with Kastner.

"Inspectors!" Kastner spotted them. "I'm so glad I don't have to call you. We are going to conduct the autopsy now."

Bri's eyebrows shot up. "Now?" She shifted her gaze to Hayes, who looked relatively sober, despite the consumption of a few beers earlier in the night. "Are you…?"

"Positive." Hayes appeared steadfast, most likely knowing what Bri was thinking.

Trent, ever the optimist, piped up, "Yeah, sure. That's great, Doc. The sooner we get the evidence, the sooner we can report to the Cap about what we're doing to solve the case." He patted Bri on the shoulder. "Right?"

"Uh, yeah, right." She tucked her hands in the pockets of her hoodie. "Sure."

Like obedient children, they trailed after Kastner and Hayes. In the suite, the body was still encased in the black bag. Hayes suited up, passing a box of gloves to Kastner and the two inspectors.

"I'll need help extracting her from the bag." She looked to Trent.

"Why not?" He stepped forward, as if she had asked him to do something as mundane as cutting the grass.

Together, they carefully shifted the body onto the metal surface of the table. The bag was then methodically rolled and placed in a large evidence container for later processing, in case something had fallen off the body during transport.

Hayes flipped on the recorder. "Initial observations of victim recovered from Islais Creek in Glen Canyon Park…" She rattled off an ID tag number as well as the date and time. "Present are Dr. Catriona Hayes, Special Agent Robert Kastner, and Inspectors Briana Ryu and William Trent."

Bri's mind drifted as Hayes continued to rattle off the details. She skimmed her gaze over the body, noting her torn sweatpants and T-shirt. Brown blood stains marred the thighs of the pants, continuing up to the apex between her thighs. Possible vicious sexual assault. She raised her eyes higher to the girl's face. Pale, blue-lipped. Blonde hair, dirty and clumped. Her eyes were closed.

"We need to cut the clothing off and bag it now." Hayes drew Bri back to the moment. She opened a kit and removed several large evidence bags. With the help of Trent, she cut the clothing from the body, the pants sticking to the victim's legs. When the girl was finally nude, a collective gasp rose in the room.

"Was she…raped?" Bri fixed her eyes on Hayes, who met the look with a mournful expression.

"I think…this is the result of a botched abortion. I'll know more when I look, but I've seen things like this when I was in Mexico…"

Hayes had spent some time in the poorer villages south of the border, where abortions were not easily accessible, and women often resorted to drastic means. Some had no choice, when there were too many mouths to feed and not enough food, or an errant spouse perhaps addicted to drugs or alcohol. It was a sad state of affairs.

"This isn't…?" Bri caught Kastner's eye across the table, speaking in hushed tones so as not to be picked up by the recorder.

"No, it doesn't match the immigration photographs of Melina Pavlok."

Bri turned back as Hayes took trace samples from the body, documenting each for later analysis. Her stomach twisted as she thought of the torture this girl must have endured. She couldn't have been older than sixteen. She should have been out with her friends, giggling about boyfriends, lamenting exams at school…but she was here. Dead.

"Fingers have been removed at the second knuckle…" Hayes opened the mouth. "All teeth have been removed. No defensive wounds that I can see." She glanced at Kastner. "Seems overkill…I mean, if the girls were trafficked into the country."

Trent interrupted, "We thought, initially, it could have been a warning to another gang, maybe?"

Bri wanted to elbow him for revealing any of their theories in the case to the Fed.

"I think you are right." Kastner crossed his arms. "While we did find your previous victim in the system, we know nothing of her. We could run it through immigration via the facial recognition database but unless someone reports her missing—which I doubt will happen—we are stuck with a Jane Doe."

"Stuck?" Bri felt heat creeping up her neck. "She's not like a nail in your tire—a mild inconvenience—she's a child. She deserves all our time and effort in finding who she is...maybe her family."

"Poor choice of words, Inspector. I apologize. I suppose after all the time I've spent watching these things happen all over the state, I've become jaded to the circumstances. You cannot get attached, as heartless as that sounds."

Trent, who was standing next to Hayes, met Bri's eyes over the table, then shifted his attention to Kastner. "Who would they be warning?" It was a purposeful shift in topic, but one which was necessary to avoid Bri shedding the Fed's blood. He really did know her well.

"Could be a rival criminal syndicate, however, there are circumstances where these organizations work together. For example, the Mafia can easily acquire blue-eyed, blonde women, who are highly valued in Asian countries. On the flip side, the Triads can obtain Asian women, who are highly valued by Eastern European men. It's a sickening partnership, but a partnership nonetheless."

Bri found herself irritated again. "Yeah, we found that out in our own research. We're not totally incompetent, ya know."

Kastner cleared his throat. "Anyway, in this case, if you're thinking it was an abortion, this may have been a warning to others not to be careless. They are merchandise, you see, and damaged merchandise doesn't sell."

"That's a fucked-up way of putting it," Hayes finally spoke, appearing to have finally become fed up with the conversation. "Now, do you want me to continue, or will you come back tomorrow...today, rather?" She made a point of looking at the clock, which showed the time as ten past midnight.

"I would like confirmation of cause of death," Bri intervened before either of the two men could contradict her.

Hayes nodded wearily. "Right. We have to wash her first." She guided Trent through the procedure, as patient as one would instruct a first-year intern. When finished, she lined up her surgical tools, picking up the scalpel and making the opening incision.

* * *

The trio exchanged no words as they exited the medical examiner's office. It was often Trent's habit to break the morbid overtones of investigations with a joke, but even he kept his lips pressed into a tight line. The horror of Dr. Hayes' autopsy findings was overwhelming. Bri looked over to Kastner, a hardened Fed, someone who dealt with human trafficking on a day to day basis, and even he appeared to be at a loss for words.

As they reached their parked vehicles, Bri finally spoke up. "There's really no use avoiding discussion of what happened in there. Maybe we should head back to the station and get a cup of coffee?" The white flag had been raised between the two investigating parties.

Kastner, in a before unseen bout of temper, kicked the wheel of his car, which must have been painful since he was wearing Oxfords. "Sonsofbitches."

Trent's eyes widened as he took a step back. "Whoa, man." He cocked his head. "Didn't know you had it in ya."

"Fucking assholes!" Kastner gave the wheel a second

kick.

At this point, Bri decided to intervene. "Yeah, we know. What they did to her…"

"Is fucking inhumane!" The profanities spewing from Kastner's lips were rapidly taking away her initial impressions of the stoic, no-nonsense Fed. A new level of respect emerged as his anger elevated.

"Yeah, we know, Agent Kastner, but you see why we have to work together? We know the city. We just need you to guide us." She hoped her outward calm would leech into Kastner. They couldn't bring a cursing Fed back to the station.

Running a hand over his hair, Kastner nodded. "You're right. I should have listened. It's just we've never seen anything of this magnitude in the state before…that girl…"

"Was brutalized, yeah."

Placing a hand to his gut, Kastner gave Bri a mournful stare. "The baby…how could someone…"

Bri wrapped her arms around her waist, meeting his eyes. "That's what we're going to find out."

15
LINA

"Wake up!"

We all sit bolt upright in bed, squinting in the harsh lights. The Big Woman, as we call her, fills the entirety of the doorway to our cramped living quarters.

"Mr. Korschev is here to speak to you."

I know that isn't his real name. As if they would tell us that, we are just lowly whores. I wrap my arms around my knees, pulling them to my chest, trying to ignore the aches in my stomach. The suited man follows Big Woman into the room, in his hand, a tan envelope. My eyes home in on it, and cold sweat drips down my spine.

"Good evening, ladies." He smiles, shark-like, his incisors gleaming.

As expected, we all respond with, "Good evening, sir."

"I am truly sorry for waking you at this late hour. I know my angels need their beauty sleep."

A memory flashes in my mind of him grunting and panting, as I tightly held the hands of one of the new girls, trying to soothe her weeping and promising it would be over soon. He was like a rutting bull, braying as he abused her. She sits on the bed next to me now, shivering. Her pain is still real; mine is dormant.

"You remember Ariadne, yes?" Her bed is neatly made still, awaiting another victim of this torment.

We nod in unison. "Yes, sir."

"She disobeyed. Took advantage of the opportunities we are giving you in this great country."

Rebellion floods my chest. So many manipulations. My voice is quickly silenced when Korschev pulls two photographs out of his pocket. He circles the room, making sure we get a good look at her mangled body.

"This is the price you will pay for disobedience. Remember, do as you're told, and your debt will be repaid in time."

Time…time is a lie in this place.

He stops in front of me, leering. "You understand, don't you, Lina?" His beefy hand caresses my cheek, stroking like one would a beloved pet.

I hate myself, but I cower, my voice not my own. "Yes, sir."

"Good."

My thoughts drift to Max, and I know this might be my only chance. "Please, sir, my brother…"

Korschev smiles. "He is on an errand. He'll be back soon." He turns. "Good night, ladies."

"Good night, sir."

The lights go off, and I can hear Big Woman and Korschev speaking in hushed tones.

"The one who asked me about her brother…bring her to me tomorrow night."

I yank the thin blanket around my trembling form and say a prayer.

16

Bri and Trent watched from the small kitchenette as Kastner sat at a desk, staring blankly ahead.

"You ever seen a Fed look that shaken up before?" Trent murmured to Bri, stirring powdered creamer into his coffee.

Soundlessly shaking her head, she continued to observe the forlorn man. "Do you have any messages from Petra Vasquez about the photograph of Max? Maybe we should run the one of Lina by her as well."

Trent nodded. "Yeah…I'll get on that now. Maybe you should go talk to him? If there was ever a man on the verge of burn out, I think our Agent Kastner fits the bill."

Bri rubbed at an invisible itch on her cheek. "Thanks for that." She picked up two mugs of coffee and headed over to Kastner. "Come on." She jerked her head in the direction of the family room, and he meekly followed. Bumping the door closed with her hip, she handed him a mug, flopping onto one of the couches.

"This is where I had my talk with Max. After he jumped out the window onto the fire escape, the chief installed a lock. Never thought anything of the window being able to open. We only usually bring families and victims in here…you know, women who've been raped or sexually assaulted. It's much more…*homey* than the interview room." In truth, Bri knew they could do better with the decorating, but in a station with limited space, it was better than nothing.

Kastner looked down at the liquid in his mug. "You must think I'm pretty pathetic."

"Shit, no. I'm admittedly surprised at your reaction—I figured a man like you must see this stuff all the time."

"The baby…"

Bri set her mug down. "Yeah…according to Hayes, it was probably alive, but they didn't…"

"Half of it was still inside her, Inspector Ryu," Kastner said bluntly. "She had cuts on her wrists and ankles. They murdered her and her child because she, no doubt, wouldn't comply with their demands to abort the baby. She must have hidden it well."

Bri thought of Max in the cold, dark freezer back in Hayes' morgue, as well as the unidentified female. Did she have someone waiting for news of her, or was she just as alone as Max and Lina?

"I'll admit, Kastner, it's fucking sick. There's no way to put it lightly." She watched his pale face, the dark circles around his eyes more prominent thanks to his complexion. "But we can do something. I need your expertise. Look, most of the time we work with straight-forward stuff, for lack of a better word. Sure, we know this shit goes on in our city, but nine times out of ten, you boys come in and knock it down before we can blink. However, this kid came to me because he thought I could help him. For whatever reason. That means he either knew who I am or there was complete desperation there."

Bri reached out, patting Kastner's shoulder. "Let us in. We have a few feelers out, but that doesn't mean anything if we're fumbling around blind."

Before Kastner could answer, a knock followed by

Trent's head poking through the door had both looking up. "Cap wants to see us."

Bri groaned, hoisting herself to her feet. "Right." As she neared the open door, Kastner's hand gently gripped her forearm.

"Inspector Ryu? If your captain approves, you can have my team's support. However, if anything goes down, you follow our lead." Passion and determination flickered in his eyes. "We'll do everything we can to rescue Max's sister, but I make no promises. Once they know we're onto them, they'll drag her into hiding or worse."

Bri nodded and he loosened his hand, following her to Captain Meyers' office.

"Shut the door, Ryu." Meyers did not look pleased to have a Fed standing in front of his desk.

Trent rested his elbow on the top of a filing cabinet, while Kastner stepped forward. "You'll have to excuse the Bureau, Captain Meyers, however, you must understand it is our duty to investigate these crimes seeing as they do fall under Federal jurisdiction in many cases. After your inspectors contacted me, I thought it best to follow up in person."

"How kind of you. The commissioner isn't too happy about the intrusion, but we'll cooperate. Trent, Ryu, hand over the case notes you've taken so far…"

Kastner held up a hand. "We'd like to work with your inspectors, Captain Meyers. This seems to be a very sophisticated syndicate with possible ties to the Mafia. Their expertise and knowledge of the city would be an invaluable resource."

Bri's mouth dropped as she locked eyes with Trent. Give Kastner his due, he could certainly weave words together in a very appealing manner, giving Meyers no possible recourse except to accept the offer on the table.

"Fine. But I want apprised of all their comings and goings. Their time is my time, Agent Kastner." Meyers absently arranged his pens in a line on his desk. "Thank you for your support."

As they were summarily dismissed from the office, Bri could barely hold back her giggles once they reached their desks. "Damn, Kastner. If I'd tried any of that, Meyers would have busted me down to meter maid. Trent here…he might have gotten away with it."

Trent was about to make a witty retort when his cell phone beeped. "Ah, shit, it's Christine. My ass is grass." He hurried off, cooing into the phone. "Christine, baby…"

Bri checked the time on her phone. "Seven am. Geez." The weight of exhaustion hit her fully and she felt her body giving into the need for sleep. "You got a place to stay, Kastner?"

The Fed straightened. "The Bureau makes sure we have houses we can stay in while on location."

"Sounds fancy. Welp, I'm headed home. If you need me, you have my number. I doubt there's much more we can do until we hear back from some of our contacts in the city."

"I'll touch base with mine. There's a Russian bistro I'd like to visit Monday night, if you'd be willing to accompany me, Inspector. The owner has worked with us in the past."

Bri's eyebrows shot up. "Why me?"

"Young, Asian, beautiful. Vasily will be falling all over himself to talk to you." Kastner grinned, the first genuine smile Bri had seen on his face since they'd met.

"Sure, but I'm not wearing a dress."

*　*　*

Bri pulled up into her designated parking space at her apartment, wearily dragging herself from the car and up the stairs. Her answering machine blinked angrily again, and due to exhaustion, instead of hitting the delete button, she hit play.

"Damn it."

Robotic voices of telemarketers informing her she'd been in a car accident and could claim personal injury now rattled on one after the other. Finally, the last message was from her mom.

"Briana, this is your mother. Can you pick up a few things on your way over today? Is that partner of yours coming? Why aren't you picking up your phone? Call me!"

Bri collapsed against the wall. She'd lost track of the days of the week again. It was Saturday. The temptation to cancel rose strongly inside her head. What time had her mother said the thing was? Begrudgingly, she picked up the phone and called her mom.

"Two o'clock, Briana. My god don't they have reminders on those cell phones?"

"Yeah, Mom, but we had a case in the early hours of this morning, then the autopsy…"

"I don't want to hear about all that blood and guts stuff, young lady. You're not calling to cancel again, are you? Nate will be so disappointed."

Nate probably wouldn't know she was even there, and he'd be so wrapped up with his latest fling, the rest of the world around him would be completely unimportant.

"I need a couple hours of sleep, and then I'll get…what did you want?"

"Two bottles of white wine, good stuff, and a pack of salad. You can handle that, can't you?"

Bri grumbled her agreement and hung up the phone, falling into bed without even bothering to change.

"Be patient with your mother, Briana. She does mean well."

The teenage Briana pouted and crossed her arms. "But, Grandpa, she just…annoys me so much."

Her grandfather smiled indulgently. "Yes, but remember, one day…she will be gone. Like I will be gone. You must learn to cherish the moments you have. You never know when something unexpected might take those we love away."

17

Petra Vasquez made her way around the shelter, checking on each girl, tucking in a blanket here, whispering a soothing word there. She knew the horrors these women had been subjected to, and she was determined to play her role in rehabilitating them, hoping the archaic practice of selling human flesh for profit would one day end.

The corners of the photograph given to her by the inspectors pressed into her flesh. The boy captured within them had her heart pang with longing—for her own little boy taken before he could even draw breath. It was the practice. Pregnant women were of little to no use to their traffickers. They often had a shady doctor on call to deal with any 'accidents.'

She massaged her temples, loosening the hair tie around her ponytail slightly. The tension headache had been building steadily since her meeting with the two inspectors. So often law enforcement approached their organization seeking help, and rarely did they give it, citing the need to keep the confidentiality of their victims. Something pulled at her, however, as she stared into the eyes of the female inspector. There was sadness, longing, and most of all, a desire to seek retribution for the poor murdered child.

She crossed the hall to the other dormitory, seeing the light coming from a propped-up flashlight of one of her girls—yes, they were her girls, and she was tasked with protecting them.

"Nadia? It's time for lights out." Petra sat on the empty cot adjacent to the girl's.

"Sorry, Ms. Vasquez, I wanted to read some more. I have my test soon."

Many of the girls were studying to complete their GED examination and gain employment. Thankfully, through the T-visa program, the girls were entitled to stay in the country as long as they agreed to work with law enforcement against their traffickers. Some were at risk of immediate danger if they were to be deported back to their home countries. Petra's ultimate goal was to see as many of her girls obtain green cards to live and work in the United States as possible, then relocate to areas where they could build lives without the fear of their traffickers finding them.

Petra watched Nadia twirl a lock of blonde hair around her finger. She was so young, only eighteen—sixteen when she had been brought here. So much of her life had been ripped away. Again, she felt the edges of the photograph jabbing her thigh.

"Nadia…if I show you a photograph, can you tell me if you know the boy in it?"

The light reflected off the girl's wide eyes. "Were the police…?"

"Yes, but I…I know I do not usually help them. However, he's young, this boy. Too young. Will you try to help me?" It was a lot to ask, and Petra held her breath.

"Sure, Ms. Vasquez. I will try."

Carefully, she withdrew the photograph from her pocket and held it out to Nadia. The girl shone her light over the pale features of the boy. "He is dead?"

Petra nodded. "Yes. Killed by someone who didn't want him found. The inspector investigating thinks he has a sister who is still there…"

"Ah! Yes! I know him."

Shock openly emanated from the woman. "You do?" It had been a million in one shot at getting a positive identification.

"Yes…Max is his name. He used to run drugs for the…people who took me. He did have a sister…Lina? I don't know. I was moved before then to a new place with a new man running things, and that's when the raid happened." She handed the picture back. "Are they going to question me? I have done well keeping things open with the police and the FBI."

"Yes, Nadia, you have. They may want to, but only if I let them."

"You can let them, Ms. Vasquez. Max was nice. He gave me chocolate once. He didn't deserve to be killed by those… *skotiny*, bastards." She clamped a hand over her mouth. "Sorry, Ms. Vasquez."

Patting the girl on the shoulder, Petra rose. "No, no, Nadia. You are quite right. They are bastards. Every last one of them. In fact, I think it is too kind a term. Lights out now and thank you."

Slipping back into the hallway, Petra exhaled, her heart still heavy after potentially putting Nadia in any danger. Retreating to the small room she kept as an office, she picked up the phone.

* * *

The beeping of her cell phone drew Bri slowly from her sleep. Checking the time, she noticed it was just past twelve. Rolling over with a groan, she answered. "Ryu."

"Hello, Inspector Ryu. This is Petra Vasquez."

All traces of exhaustion left Bri's body in anticipation of what Petra had to say. "Yes, hello." She swung her legs over the edge of the bed.

Silence, punctuated by a shaky intake of breath. Bri thought Petra had hung up before she began to speak. "I have a girl at my shelter…she knew your victim, Max."

Petra now had Bri as a captive audience. "She knew him?" Bri was aware she was sounding like a parrot, but with her memory of Petra being so protective over her girls, she wasn't sure if asking to speak to the one who had identified Max would provoke a positive response.

"Yes…and she said she would speak to you and your partner…away from the police station, of course."

"Of course." The weight on Bri's shoulders lightened considerably. "Where would she like to meet us?"

"I will talk to her this evening and give you a call."

"Wonderful, Ms. Vasquez, thank you so much. I understand this goes against your personal ethics, and, well, I just wanted to say how much I appreciate your help." Bri hoped she was adequately conveying her feelings on the matter. While empathetic, she did have a case to solve and she was glad that Petra and this girl were cooperating.

"Goodbye, Inspector."

Placing the phone on the bed, Bri did a little celebratory dance, something she usually only kept in her head. Then she texted Trent on the way to the bathroom for a quick shower before she headed off to her mother's.

Got info re: Max from Vasquez. To meet ASAP.

It didn't take long for the reply. *K. Kastner still hanging around. Pissing off Cap. What should I do with him?*

Bri's thumbs hovered over the screen. Was it really wise to do what she was thinking? Ah, hell, maybe it would take the Fed's mind off things for a bit.

Mom's having a party. Said you should come. Bring the Fed.
K.

Setting the phone on the cabinet by the bathroom door, Bri was washed in a wave of regret, and the horror of having both Trent and Kastner in her mother's clutches settled in her stomach like a lead weight. "Ah, shit. What have I done?"

18

"Briana! Good. You brought what I asked you to. I was thinking you would forget." Her mother, Marian, brown hair cut in a fashionable bob, came up to her daughter's chin. She took the bag into the kitchen.

Walking into the open plan living and dining room, Bri cast a glance around at the gathered parties, relieved to see her partner and the Fed hadn't arrived yet. The small suburban neighborhood had been ideal while Bri was growing up, the elementary school just a few blocks down the street and the middle school and high school a convenient bus ride away. Her father was a retired police officer, and her mother spent most of her time volunteering with local organizations.

Lowering herself to the couch next to her dad, John, he smiled, wrapping her in a one-armed hug. At a height of six-foot-three and with a large build, her dad often intimidated people, but she knew he was just a big teddy bear. "You're the first person here, Bri baby. Your brother and sister got held up in traffic. An accident on the 101." Her father hated stupid drivers with a passion.

"Oh, uh, that's good. Hey, I wanted to tell you that Trent decided to come after all and, uh, well, we have a visiting Fed who…sorta needed time to kill."

"That's fine. Luckily, we're having some sun today, so I took out the BBQ."

As Bri had traveled away from the city, the weather had brightened from the gloomy overcast. It would be Thanksgiving soon, another occasion for all the family to get together at her grandmother's house, but it wouldn't be the same without her grandfather—it never was.

"So, a visiting Fed, eh?"

Bri cozied back into the recliner, angling her eyes up to the white ceiling. "Yeah…we caught a case involving human trafficking, but…"

"…that's all you can say. I understand." He nodded, turning off the TV and hoisting himself off the couch. As he did, a knock sounded at the door.

Bri peered around her father as he answered the door, catching sight of Trent and Kastner, the latter looking incredibly sheepish.

"Hey, Billy, good to see you." The pair stepped into the house, and John shook Trent's hand.

"You too, Mr. Ryu. It's been a while."

"Yeah, yeah, it has. Head into the kitchen and grab a beer. I know Marian will want to give you the once over."

Trent sidled his way past the welcoming committee, shooting Bri a look, followed by a grin. She stuck her tongue out at him as he leaned in. "What were you thinking? Temporary insanity?"

Before she could throw a punch at his arm, he danced off to the kitchen.

"Uh, right, Dad, this is Agent Robert Kastner, Kastner, this is my dad. John Ryu."

"Nice to meet you, sir. Thanks for inviting me on such short notice." Kastner stuck out his hand. Bri was amused at his choice of attire, surprised the Fed traveled with khakis and a polo in his overnight bag. Then again, she was used to Kastner throwing surprises her way after their conversation at the station.

"Likewise. Same goes. Beer in the fridge. I'm gonna go start up the BBQ before your mother gets irritated." Her dad clapped a hand on Bri's shoulder before disappearing out the sliding glass door.

Bri was left alone with Kastner in an awkward 'don't-know-what-to-say' position.

"This was unexpected." Kastner finally broke the ice. He appeared more composed than when they had parted last night.

"Well, sometimes, you need a dose of normality in the face of hellish circumstances."

Kastner shifted his weight. "So, Inspector Trent tells me you heard back from Petra Vasquez?"

"I did, but no shop talk. I'll fill you in on Monday at the station, if that's okay." She frowned as Kastner peered around the room. "Uh, do you have family? Prewarning, mine is kinda crazy."

"No, not really. I guess I'm what they would describe as married to the job. My parents had me when they were older so they both passed away about five years ago." His face belied no hint of emotion, and Bri decided not to pry as Trent returned with three beers, passing them around.

"Your mom still thinks we should hook up. A baseball bat to the head would have been more subtle."

"Also might've knocked some sense into you." Bri wrinkled her nose.

Kastner let out a laugh, drawing the surprised attention of Bri and Trent. "So, he does have a sense of humor," Trent joked, clapping Kastner on the back. "Relax, man, we're off-duty."

He cleared his throat, taking a small sip of beer. "Yeah, it's hard to switch off sometimes."

Marian bustled into the living room. "Come on, you three! Oh, who's this?" She fixed Bri with one of the stares she got when she had a glimmer of hope of marrying her daughter off.

"Mom, Agent Robert Kastner of the FBI. Kastner, this is my mom, Marian."

"Welcome! Your father didn't tell me we had another guest here." She looped her arm through Kastner's. "Come help me set the table."

Bri shot Trent a 'help me' look, and he just laughed. "Not my circus, not my monkeys."

She mouthed the words, *Fuck you*.

"I'm telling!" Trent teased, just as the door burst open, and the rest of the horde arrived.

***

Dinner wound down, and Bri, Trent, and Kastner sat outside in the rapidly cooling evening air, the silence a comforting blanket around the trio. Everyone, save Bri's parents, obviously, had departed in a flurry of hugs and shouts of goodbye. Tomorrow was Sunday, and while it might not prove to be the lazy day most people in the rest of the world thought of it as, laughter and family would at least provide a cushion to whatever might come along.

Bri's cell chose that moment to vibrate to life as a text message popped up on the screen from Petra.

Golden Gate Park. Botanical Gardens. Tomorrow 2pm. Just you.

19

The gray clouds pressed down, threatening rain, as they had done for most of the week. Trent initially objected to Bri going alone, but when Kastner remarked that the witness might feel better speaking to a woman, he quieted, resolving to remain at the car with Kastner hovering in the backseat, both eagerly awaiting any snippet of evidence.

On the way over, Kastner reminded her of the visit to the Russian bistro. His momentary lapse into relaxation had ended that morning when they got into the station. It was all business again. While they waited for two pm to hit, Kastner went into Meyers' office and cleared the use of Bri for the undercover operation the following night. Meyers was apparently reluctant, which gave Bri some consolation that he might actually care about what happened to her. However, he approved it, saying they better come up information they could use instead of running around like 'headless fucking chickens.'

"He really does expect a high turn around. For all the progress we've made in the past four days, you'd think he'd be grateful," Kastner had muttered.

"I get it. Two bodies in nearly as many days? He's just

waiting for the third and then the press shitstorm that is going to come down on us like a ton of bricks." There was no disagreeing with Trent's consensus. Things had the potential to get worse. All three were hoping that Petra Vasquez's witness might hold the missing key.

Bri exited the vehicle as Kastner rolled down the window.

"I still think we should have put a mic on you…"

"She's an eighteen-year-old victim, Kastner…not some thug with a gun in his waistband." She turned without further discussion and made her way through the parking lot toward the gate, taking a right down the path. Petra had told her they would be in the Moon Viewing Garden when she'd texted to confirm the meeting that morning.

As Bri approached, she noticed a slight blonde girl standing next to the taller Petra. Both were leaning on the edge of the wooden dock, looking out across the various plants and trees in the gardens. She cleared her throat so as not to startle them.

Petra turned and smiled. "Inspector Ryu."

The girl next to her couldn't have been older than eighteen, her large eyes fixed on Bri, taking in every detail meticulously, belying her cautious nature and quite understandable in the circumstances she must have faced.

"This is Nadia."

Bri held out her hand to the young woman, and she grasped it tentatively before releasing it.

"Hello, Inspector Ryu." Her voice was soft, words precise, with the hint of an Eastern European accent.

"I appreciate you meeting with me, Nadia. I can appreciate how difficult this must be."

She let out a laugh. "You speak like a police officer."

Glancing to Petra, Bri flushed. She refocused on Nadia. "Sorry…old habits die hard."

"We can sit on that bench, if you wish." Nadia

motioned to one alongside the path, her blonde hair swishing as she turned her head.

"If that's…" Bri almost slipped back into her 'interviewing victims' mode. She caught herself and nodded. "Sure."

The group of women moved to the bench, sitting, with Nadia between Petra and Bri. Bri bounced her leg, trying to think of the best way to commence without it coming across like an interrogation.

"Nadia…Petra, erm, Ms. Vasquez said you recognized the boy in the photograph. Can you tell me how you knew him?"

A distant, detached expression cloaked Nadia's face. Bri peered over at Petra, trying to check in and make sure Nadia was okay. Petra gave her a subtle nod and placed a reassuring hand on Nadia's shoulder. The young woman's eyes clouded, mimicking the weather, before clearing.

"I remember seeing Max once. He came into the room where all the girls were kept by the traffickers. He went to see one particular girl. At first, we joked—silly, I know to think that some of the girls joked, but it was how we coped. There were a few different ways of coping…but I digress. Anyway, we found out that Lina, the girl he came to see, was his sister. It soon became clear to many of us that they were brought here together."

Although many of the flowers weren't blooming, Bri was sure she caught a subtle fragrance on the breeze that gently rustled her hair. She breathed in deeply, centering herself once again. "Did Max ever speak to you?"

"No. He hardly spoke to anyone, aside from Lina. There were times we didn't know where we were, they moved us so often and kept the décor relatively plain. I know now it was to keep us disorientated so we didn't focus on escape…they stripped all hope from us."

Bri inwardly cursed. She had hoped for some hint, anything really, to indicate where the young women had been held. "Do you remember any sounds? Maybe the traffickers speaking…"

"I'm sorry, Inspector Ryu," Nadia interrupted. "The other inspectors who interviewed me in Oakland asked me this before. It was luck that I was in the house they raided. This was after I was sold to another." Her face screwed up in disgust, likely at the prospect of being treated like human chattel.

Bri switched tactics. "Who were you…" She struggled for the proper word, but in the end, decided to mimic Nadia. "…sold to?"

"When you're ordered to remain silent, sometimes all you can do is listen. That is, if you don't retreat into yourself. I was traded to an Asian man. I remember them speaking in a different language, like the Russian men did…"

"You knew they were Russian?"

"Yes. Although Ukrainian and Russian sound similar, as do most of the Eastern European languages, there are distinctions. Anyway, I heard them mention Triad. It was only later through Petra that I learned that the Triads are another organized crime gang who operate all over the world."

"It makes sense based on our investigations. Were a lot of women traded to them?"

"Occasionally they would have parties and invite these men. It was there that they would choose who they favored for their own establishments."

Petra broke into the conversation. "Some of the survivors won't remember as much detail. Many of them disassociate from what is happening. We've worked with a few who have suffered from DID."

"Dissociative Identity Disorder? You mean they have…"

"Multiple personalities, yes. It's not uncommon with prolonged traumatic experiences."

Nadia stared off again, her eyes moving over the plants and up into the trees. "I don't have DID, but many of the girls I knew went into child-like states after the abuse they suffered. Some grew angry, protective."

Bri bit her tongue, wanting to ask about the female they had in the morgue.

Nadia clocked her immediately. "Please, ask, Inspector. I have been a survivor for nearly a year now. I am studying to get a good education and go to college. The charity is helping me change my name as well so they will never be able to find me."

"We have another young woman in the morgue at the moment. She was pregnant shortly before her death and it appears that…she was forced to undergo an abortion."

Nadia nodded as if the statement was in reference to something completely mundane. "Ah, yes, pregnancy takes away the value of the woman. A trafficker cannot use a pregnant slave, can he?"

"It appears she fought…"

"Yes, some would. Some would resign themselves to the procedure peacefully. It…depended."

"Is there anything else you can tell me? We want to find Lina, if at all possible." Bri already appeared to know the answer before Nadia even spoke.

"If I could, I would rescue every girl trapped there, Inspector. It was…odd to see a teenage boy amongst the women. While men are trafficked, yes, they know women are easier to control and are of greater value. I often wondered about Max myself, but when you are in these situations, you look out for yourself. Maybe find the reason Max was trafficked with Lina, and you might have an answer."

Petra wrapped an arm around Nadia's shoulders. "You did well. Can I speak to the inspector for a few moments alone?"

Nadia gave Bri a smile and stood. "I hope you find

her, Inspector. I know it is unlikely, but I still have hope." Her footsteps retreated, crunching along the path away from Petra and Bri.

When some distance was established between the women and Nadia, Petra angled her body to Bri. "The girl you mentioned…what happened? I sense there was more than what you were willing to reveal in front of Nadia."

Bri locked her brown eyes on Petra's, sensing that the woman wouldn't be pawned off with any type of half-assed answer. "The…poor infant…was dismembered."

Petra's hand flew to her mouth. "Those monsters."

"The female experienced massive internal bleeding. She was restrained."

"My God." Petra crossed herself, causing Bri's eyes to widen. She hadn't realized the woman was Catholic.

"Yeah, I…we don't know how to proceed with that investigation, so we're hoping the investigation into Max's death will lead to clues about who the poor young woman was."

Petra's hand landed on top of Bri's. "Please…do all you can. Don't let her become another nameless statistic."

The palm resting on the back of her hand was strangely comforting, and a warmth began to blossom in Bri's chest. She quashed it, knowing that becoming attached to someone who was a part of an active investigation was dangerous. Add to that the fact she didn't know if Petra was merely being kind or if she had the same proclivities as Bri. She knew better than to assume everyone did. It was worthwhile to be cautious always.

"I will do my best. We have an FBI agent down from Sacramento. We're hoping his connections will get us some answers." It was about all she could reveal about the ongoing investigation without potentially compromising it.

With a gentle pat, Petra lifted her hand. "I am glad."

The warmth subsided as Petra stood up, and an aching pang was left in its place. "You have a kind way about you, Inspector Ryu. You read the cues from Nadia and adjusted your questions accordingly. Not many law enforcement officers have that ability. If you do find Lina, please call me. I want to help." A smile crossed her lips as she nodded. "Goodbye for now, Inspector." She walked with purpose away from the bench, following the same path taken by Nadia.

Bri remained sitting long after Petra's form retreated into the distance. There were few people in the gardens that day, probably on account of the threatening rain. Her cell buzzed in her pocket, and she retrieved it, glancing at the screen as the first drop of rain blurred the text. She swiped it away with a thumb.

All good? Trent was checking in. It was then Bri noted that she had been there for over an hour.

Yeah, all good. Coming now.

K. Gotta get ready for your debut.

Bri inwardly grimaced. Kastner had mentioned wanting to brief her for the following night when all she really wanted to do was sleep. The investigation was beginning to take a heavy emotional toll on her, especially after speaking with Nadia. What if they never found Lina? What if this became the case which would haunt her throughout her career?

Standing, she shook her head vigorously. No, she would not fall into melancholy at the thought of failure. It simply wasn't an option. They had to find Lina.

20
LINA

I stand by his office door, waiting, an obedient puppy unsure if I will be received well or struck. Such is the nature of the abusive cycle I have found myself in. What I would have done differently before Leon filled my head with colorful lies haunts me daily. What if our parents hadn't died in an accident? Would this have still happened? Maybe Max would have been left safely at home, and I would have fallen into this trap alone.

That's what it is—a trap. A woven web of promises, with a spider at the center, waiting to strike, its venom delivering you back to reality.

"Come!" His voice, emotionless, calls out and I jump. My legs won't move. Why won't they move? MOVE!

"Are you going to stand there like a mindless *pizda*, or are you going to come when I call you?"

I despise that word—*pizda*. There is nothing more derogatory in the Russian language to call a woman. That horrible word. The English translation blares in my head. Cunt. That's all we are to them.

My stomach rumbles, reminding me that my weakness

comes from lack of nutrition. Finally, I move, knowing that disobedience leads to punishment.

"Ah, you do have ears. Sit there." He points to a wooden chair alongside his desk. I will my knees not to collapse as I lower myself down. I can see the bones in my knees. How can men find this body attractive or desirable?

"Your brother…"

My spine straightens. I am strong. For Max, I am strong.

"Has disappeared."

My inner bundle of strength fades. I forget myself. "I…don't understand…"

"Are you dumb too? He has disappeared. Now, you are responsible for both debts. We didn't bring you to this country to get a free ride." He is writing on a piece of paper, not even meeting my eyes.

No, you brought me here to be a slave. There is no end to my debts; there never will be. I refrain from speaking my true thoughts. "No, sir." The title comes easily to my lips. Max…Max…where have you gone? Have you sought help? Is that why you abandon me?

"You will work a party this weekend. Go tell Sasha to feed you. Don't forget you are nothing."

He will work me to death now. No, don't think like that. Max isn't dead. He's just disappeared. Disappeared means they don't know where he is. I will work. I will keep my mind active and strong.

"Are you waiting for permission? Go!"

His voice makes me jolt. "Thank you, sir." I hurry from the room, the prospect of a hot meal spurning me on. Max is alive, I repeat to myself. He will find me.

21

"You have to have some surveillance of these rings in the city, I mean, come on. San Francisco is too big not to be a focus of the Bureau's attention!" After her meeting with Petra and Nadia, Bri's temper flared unexpectedly once they arrived back at the station. "It can't be that no one knows anything!"

"Inspector Ryu, we do what we can, but some of these operations are extremely covert. We don't know how many are even operating in the city alone."

"What do you know?" Bri shrugged off Trent's hand, momentarily feeling guilty for pushing him aside. Everyone was working hard and didn't deserve this outburst.

Trent persevered. "It's only been a week, Bri...less than that. You know investigations take time. We still don't have trace back from Max and the female victim. Maybe that will give us a clue as to where they were kept. Yelling at Kastner isn't going to solve anything."

Her temper fizzled as she was admonished. Kastner sat sheepishly at her desk. "Sorry...I...talking to Nadia, knowing what she must have gone through and knowing that Lina is probably facing the same things is really pushing me to move quickly."

Kastner nodded. "I do understand, Inspector. I promise you; I do. We're not all cold-hearted suits at the Bureau. We do our best with the information we are given. Let's focus on one step at a time. For the moment, we can look at what's going to happen tomorrow night."

Bri rubbed her hands on her pants, before hoisting her frame onto the edge of her desk, pushing aside a few errant pens and pieces of paperwork. "Okay."

Kastner produced the image of a clean-cut, suited man. "Vasily Sokolov. He owns the Little Russian Tea Room. After we busted him for tax evasion, he made a deal to work with us based on certain information he was privy to regarding trafficking rings. I suspect he's held onto it for some time, knowing this was coming. Since then, he's provided us with credible intel which has led to several raids. His information is sporadic, to prevent him from being found out and eliminated by the Mafia, Triads, or both. He usually contacts us, but I thought we would make an exception in this case."

Bri scanned the photograph again. He was probably in his early fifties, every inch the sophisticated businessman. "Why would the Mafia trust him with information?"

"We make certain allowances."

"You're gonna have to elaborate, Kastner. I'm not going in blind."

"Drugs, Inspector. We allow him to run drugs." Kastner appeared despondent by the revelation, as if it disgusted him to admit that the Bureau would sacrifice one crime for another.

"The same drugs some of these traffickers use to subdue their victims…the same drugs found in Max?" Bri's neck heated. Trent caught her eye, giving an unwritten warning to remain in control.

"Yes, I'm sorry to say. But we control the flow. And it

all flows through the Little Russian Tea Room." Kastner said this as if it was a small consolation.

Bri scoffed. "Sure."

"Anyway, we have contacted Sokolov through our means and he replied, as you know, that tomorrow night would be suitable. I would ask a few things from you, Inspector Ryu, when we go."

"You can ask, but it's up in the air whether or not I'll be okay with it."

Trent butted in. "If it means finding Lina, didn't you say you'd do anything?"

The look of death Bri gave to Trent had him visibly recoiling. "Yes, I did…or words to that effect."

"Then maybe we should just do as Kastner advises in this case. You'll have a wire, and I won't look down on you for being obedient, for once." Trent recovered quickly and resumed his joking manner.

"Fine." Bri knew she was pouting, and she despised it. "What do I need to do?"

* * *

That evening, over empty cartons of Chinese food, Bri, Trent, and Hayes sat around, nursing cold beers. The calm before the storm, Hayes had joked when she came to the little pow-wow. Kastner had pled out, saying he needed to check in with his supervisor before tomorrow night's operation at the Little Russian Tea Room. Bri was pretty sure he'd had enough socialization to last him a lifetime after the previous night's gathering at her parents' house.

"He's a strange one, isn't he?" Hayes spoke up, tracing her fingertip over a spot of moisture on her beer bottle.

Trent lifted his eyes, taking a swig. "Kastner? Yeah…sorta. I guess that type of profession would attract weirdos. Never liked Feds. Too much starch under the collar."

"He's not that bad." Bri's comment had both staring at her with open mouths. "What?"

"Not that bad? Who are you, and what have you done with my partner?" Trent shook her shoulder gently with a laugh.

Bri swatted him away. "Hey, it's not like he has it easy, you know. Seeing all those victims…far from home, betrayed…burn out is real."

"Ooo, look at you getting all psychological on us." Hayes grinned and placed her empty bottle on the table, before standing to get another.

"It's not…I mean…ugh!" Bri crossed her arms, huffing like a teenager who had just been told they were grounded.

Hayes laughed as she returned with a new round. "Oh, Bri, my love, you gotta lighten up. You're easier to get a rise out of than anyone I know."

"I feel like we're running blind here." There it was—her admission of potential failure looming in the distance, an executioner's blade ready to fall.

Trent scratched the back of his head. "Isn't that how we always are? Fumbling around in the dark until we get bitten?"

"Yeah, but if I didn't know Max from before, he'd have just been another nameless statistic."

Hayes rested a hand on her shoulder, landing on the couch beside her. "You can't be so brutal on yourself, Bri. The point isn't what might have happened, it's what did happen." She dropped her head to Bri's shoulder. "So, focus on moving forward. Later, once you've found Lina…" Bri opened her mouth to interrupt, but Hayes held up a hand. "…as I said, *once* you've found Lina, we can untangle all the philosophical questions of the universe, deal?"

Hayes' hair smelled of citrus, something she put in

her shampoo to get rid of the ever-present smell of death which circled her. Bri turned her head to Trent and saw he was bobbing his in agreement. "Well, I can't compete with two against one." She wrinkled her nose as Trent put a cold pot sticker into his mouth.

"What? Food is food, Ryu."

"And yet, you never gain a pound. What excuse did you use for Christine tonight?"

"Uh, Christine...yeah, we called it quits for good this time."

Hayes and Bri exchanged looks. "Uh huh," Bri said.

Trent straightened. "No, I mean it. Shit, all my overtime pay goes to making it up to her for not being there." His shoulders drooped. "And...well..."

"Go on," Hayes prompted.

"Ah, hell, she was cheating on me, okay?"

Bri's eyes widened. "What? The infallible Christine?"

Trent dropped his eyes. "So...I came home the other night...you know, when we were waiting for results and shit and...I found another guy's shirt in my closet. She tried to tell me it was mine, but I don't wear American Eagle." He made a face. "Besides, it was time, ya know?"

Hayes leaned over and tapped her beer bottle to his. "Congratulations. We were wondering when you'd see the light."

"Huh?"

"You're too good for her, Billy. Come on! She was always complaining. You never really enjoyed being in a relationship with her. You enjoyed the idea of it." Hayes arched a perfect ebony eyebrow. "Am I wrong?"

Trent set his face into a sulk. "Damn women." His rapid change of subject had Bri and Hayes stifling giggles. "What about tomorrow night...Kastner...think he can remove the stick from his ass to be believable?"

Bri let the cool beer fizzle down her throat. "Yeah, I think so."

His expression grew serious. "First sign of trouble, you're outta there, Bri, okay? No bullshit."

Opening her mouth to argue, Bri rapidly closed it. Trent didn't mess around when it came to looking after her, nor would she, if he had been in the same situation. "No bullshit."

The rest of the evening progressed with lighter topics of conversation and joking, but inside, Bri remained somber, wondering what tomorrow would bring, hopefully taking them one step closer to Lina and her silent promise to help Max find his sister. When she said goodnight to Hayes and Trent, her bed did little to provide any comforting reprieve from her troubled thoughts, and her dreams swirled with darkening clouds. Suddenly, they cleared.

"Bri, things will push at you, pummel you, make you feel like giving up, but you can't." Her grandfather's kindly smile broke through.

"I...can't."

"You can. You will bend, Briana Ryu, but you will never break."

22

Vasily Sokolov had sequestered himself in one of the dimly lit booths at the back of his restaurant. He prided himself on a well-run business, knowing that all the right connections made the difference between success and failure. As he skimmed a finger over the books from the previous week, he flicked open the button at the collar of his pressed white shirt, loosening his tie first. Without a need for prompting, a waitress brought him a whiskey sour, his favorite drink.

He let a manicured finger drift over the numbers, the carefully recorded receipts and the invoices. There had been an unusually large bill paid the previous evening, but he was expecting it. However, if the IRS were ever to come calling, they would see that the men who left the sizable tip only had a round of drinks. Such was the business. He allowed the Mafia to run cocaine and heroin through his business, and he reaped the rewards, to a point. An unlucky brush with the law had left him at the behest of the FBI, something he begrudgingly accepted in exchange for information.

The smooth whiskey trickled down his throat and warmed his chest. Unencumbered with the restrains of family, Sokolov enjoyed the finer things in life to the fullest, and even at fifty-two, he still considered himself a virile specimen of the male species. He kept a cool head, even in the most irritating of situations...except when he received a call from Agent Kastner. His first instinct was to tell the sanctimonious prick where to go, but the interior of a prison cell still lacked appeal.

Yet, the niggling question remained—why had Kastner contacted him? In the past, their symbiotic relationship had been quite simple: he would provide information on any trafficked girls, and Kastner would continue to allow the drug income to trickle in, so long as Sokolov did not take advantage of the situation. Perhaps there was a specific girl he was interested in this time. The prospects tantalized Sokolov to no end, and his curiosity piqued considerably.

"Mr. Sokolov, there is a man here to see you." One of the hosts had cautiously approached the table. Sokolov, while a fair employer, was known for his hair-trigger temper, and no one wanted to be on the wrong side of it when it went off. He had his routine, and his routine had just been interrupted.

"You know I have reserved this time especially for my own purposes." His accent shone through as he felt his temperature rising. Since his parents had brought him to San Francisco in the late seventies, he had done his utmost to blend in with the new world. But, in those rare moments, he could revert to his native tongue faster than one could blink.

"I know, Mr. Sokolov, sir, but he was insistent. He said you would be interested in some *merchandise*?"

The code word had his temper receding. He downed the rest of the drink to bolster his confidence and waved a ringed hand. "Show him over."

The host scampered off and returned not a moment later with a suited man, his dark hair slicked back with enough gel to skate on. "Vasily, it is good to see you, my friend."

Recognizing the man immediately, Sokolov rose from his booth, clasping his hand. "Andrei! What can I do for you this evening? Wait, first, would you like something to eat, a drink? It must be very late for you."

Korschev waved a hand. "No, no, please."

"I must insist. A drink, then. Your usual dry martini, one olive, one onion?" He snapped his fingers and the same waitress from before went to retrieve it from the bartender. Sokolov prided himself on anticipating the needs of his guests.

Korschev relented. "Ah, yes, fine, fine. Shall we sit, old friend?" Without waiting for further invitation, he heaved his corpulent form into the soft velveteen seat.

Sokolov hesitantly shifted into the seat opposite him, waiting patiently for Korschev to elaborate on the reason for his visit, and he knew through instinct that this wasn't going to end up being something beneficial for him.

"You have been quite loyal, have you not, Vasily?"

He stiffened at the use of his proper name. "I have done my best to provide a good service, when required." His gray eyes skimmed the room, making sure that there were no eavesdroppers.

"It is time for me to ask a favor of you that goes beyond our usual transactions." Korschev folded his hands over the straining buttons of his dress shirt. He paused as the waitress brought forth the martini, not spilling a drop of the clear liquid. She also placed a fresh drink before Sokolov, scurrying away to other duties. She was a good girl, Galena, Sokolov's niece on his wife's side, working her way through college. He always made sure she had enough in tips to enjoy the little extras life afforded them. He didn't want to get on the bad side of his wife.

Sokolov smiled congenially. "Of course, old friend.

Anything to be of service."

"I was hoping you would say that." A shark-tooth smile was issued in return. "I have a girl I need held for a few days, until I can relocate her. Do you think you are able to accommodate this request?"

A hidden shiver traversed Sokolov's spine. He did not agree so much with Korschev's other business practices. He preferred his women willing, discrete, and pliable. However, saying that, he was sure he had been offered one of Korschev's girls on occasion to keep him under his thumb.

"Why, of course, Andrei, it would be my distinct privilege to help you out." Sokolov took a larger than usual mouthful of his drink, attempting to hide the building cough in his throat. "When would you like me to…you know."

"As soon as possible. Tonight, perhaps?"

This time, Sokolov did choke. "Tonight? I…am deeply sorry, old friend, but I am entertaining guests for the evening. Perhaps I could have something arranged by the middle of the week?"

Korschev strummed his fingers on the table, the concussive tempo creating delicate ripples along the liquid surface of his drink. "I suppose I might put up with her for a few more days."

Bowing his head, Sokolov openly displayed his difference and gratitude, while at the same time, his inner self was panicking, thinking of Agent Kastner and his unexpected request to meet tomorrow night. Was it connected? He hoped to God it was not.

Korschev downed the martini in a single gulp, tugging the olive and onion off the swizzle stick with his blindingly white teeth. "Very good. There will be a significant tip coming your way." He hoisted his body out of the booth, looking in the direction of Sokolov's niece, who was playing on her iPhone. "Your waitress is lovely."

"Yes, family business, you know. My wife insisted," Sokolov blurted out.

"Ah, yes, wives. I never saw much need for one. But I imagine she keeps a good house for you, no?"

"The best. She is a wonderful mother. My son's wife is expecting their first child soon. She is elated with the prospect of becoming a grandmother." The relief that the topic had shifted was palpable.

Korschev clapped Sokolov on the shoulder. "I will be in touch in a few days, Vasily." He moved toward the door, pausing and turning. "Do not disappoint me." And with those ominous words, he departed.

Sokolov felt all tension dissolve from his muscles as he sat again. What was he getting into?

23

"No. Absolutely not. There is no possible way." Bri crossed her arms, frowning at Kastner and the little brown bag he now held aloft in her direction.

"Inspector Ryu, I must insist. Sokolov already knows I'm with the Bureau. I want to keep your reputation away from the realm of law enforcement. If he thinks I'm slipping, he might be more forthcoming."

"My reputation? Ha! I put that…thing on, and my reputation is the last thing I have to worry about."

Trent, sitting on Bri's desk, could barely contain his chuckling until Bri glared at him with such ferocity, he actually blanched. "Why don't you…uh…ask Hayes to help you?"

"Cat…Dr. Hayes has enough on her plate with two bodies sitting in the morgue from our investigation, on top of her usual workload." It was a half-hearted excuse—Bri knew Hayes would jump at the opportunity.

"I'm calling her." Trent pulled out his cell, and Bri grabbed for it, but he dodged her. Sometimes, she forgot he had played high school football and had been a star quarterback for his team, used to dodging people who tried to get in his way.

"Hi, Cat…it's Billy. Yeah, I have something I need you to help me with…"

"No, no, no!" Bri shouted and made a second pass for the cell. By this point, they had everyone in the office watching the exchange between the pair. A small crowd was gathering, including Captain Meyers, whose perturbed look sent a few officers scurrying.

"…Bri needs some help with a dress…"

"I HATE YOU! I'm not a Barbie doll!" Bri gave up and groaned. Kastner simply blinked, obviously not used to seeing this sort of scene between law enforcement officers.

"…Great, see you in twenty." Trent grinned at Bri. "It's done. Hayes is more than happy to help with this little project."

"I *really* hate you."

"No, you don't, you love me." Trent plucked the brown bag out of Kastner's hand, fishing out the flimsy black fabric far enough to read the label. He stared at Kastner incredulously. "How'd you guess her size?"

Bri narrowed her eyes. "It's my *size*?"

The special agent turned all shades of red in the span of thirty seconds. "I…guessed."

Trent clutched his stomach, crinkling the bag in the process. "He guessed! I love it. This is too rich." He waved a hand to the spectators. "Bets are on! How long before Ryu kills the Fed? Odds are ten to one on 'soon.'"

Meyers cleared his throat. "That's enough tomfoolery for one day. Back to work everyone. Agent Kastner, I'd like to clarify a few details for tonight." Then, in a rare spat of humor, he looked to Bri. "Inspector Ryu, you may have the rest of the afternoon off, paid, to…prepare for your undercover operation."

Bri shot daggers at Kastner. "You know, Trent is right. I don't hate him. I hate *you*."

Kastner's mouth opened and closed like a landed fish

and then he trailed after Meyers to his office, the door shutting with an audible click.

"Mature, Ryu," Trent murmured into her ear.

"Oh…shut up." She snatched the bag off him. "I'll wait for Hayes downstairs…away from the peanut gallery!" At that, the final few officers scattered, none wanting to get in the path of the angry inspector.

***

When Hayes walked through the front door of reception, Bri glanced up, looking completely dejected. "This is so not my thing, Cat."

Hayes sat next to her friend. "I know, and Billy told me you threw a major hissy fit in the middle of the precinct."

"I did not…well, okay, I did." Bri had reduced the paper bag in her lap to a crinkled mess. "I just don't do dresses…or hair…or make-up."

Hayes patted her shoulder. "But this is for your job and I know you want to see Lina rescued as much as anyone up there. So, when we want something more than anything, we tend to go outside our comfort zone. Now, come on. I've made an appointment for you at my hairdresser, and we'll get your nails done as well, same place. Nothing too fancy, just a manicure. I know you'd hate fake ones." She held out her hand. "Let me see the dress."

Bri reluctantly handed over the bag, and Hayes peeled it open, pulling out a black mini-dress. "This is…actually really chic, Bri. Who got it?"

"Kastner."

Hayes' eyebrows arched. "Agent Kastner? Stuffy Special Agent Kastner? Damn. Who knew the guy had taste?"

"I know, right?" Bri managed a small smile, finally standing. "Let's get this over with. At least I'm getting

105

paid."

Hayes linked her arm through Bri's. "Paid salon days. If only the taxpayers knew."

As they exited onto Vallejo Street, Bri stopped abruptly, causing Hayes to jerk back. "What?"

"It feels wrong, Cat. Going to do this while Lina…"

"Don't even say it, Bri. We both know this is a means to an end, hopefully." Hayes patted her hand.

"How do we know that, though? What if this meeting tonight leads to nothing?" Overwhelming doubt flooded Bri. It was the first time she'd ever felt such a lack of confidence in herself and her investigation. Was she getting emotionally attached?

Hayes faced Bri, ignoring all the grumbling pedestrians who had to circumvent them. "Briana Ryu, you are the most competent and intelligent inspector I know. If anyone can get the answers, it's you. You're ruthless. It's what makes you so good at your job. It's the added personal touch. Sure, I think because you think you failed Max in the first place, you have an obligation to get this case solved, but that's okay. Don't worry. If Trent or I saw you were getting in too deep, we'd pull you back. Got it?"

Bolstered by a Catriona Hayes pep talk, Bri nodded. "Got it." Her friend was right. She did feel a sense of obligation to Max, but she had to maintain her perspective.

"Good." Hayes returned to her side and they progressed along to the salon Hayes had chosen.

As soon as Bri entered, she was hit with the overwhelming smell of acetone and hairspray. Somehow, she favored the smells of the morgue. These were unfamiliar and reminiscent of her high school prom, when her mother had subjected her to dresses and updos. A bubbly blonde in a black smock greeted Hayes like an old friend, before beginning her inspection of Bri, clicking her tongue as she circled.

"At least she has amazing skin and bone structure. Her hair is gorgeous too! What do you use on it?"

Bri blinked. "Shampoo?"

The blonde let out a tinkling laugh. "Oh, she's a hoot! Let's get you in the chair. What about the other things we discussed?" She glanced to Hayes conspiratorially.

"What other things?" Bri strained to turn her head toward the women.

"We'll deal with those after." Hayes sat in a hot pink chair in the waiting area, picking up a *People* magazine.

The blonde, who Bri found out was called Kirsty, washed and straightened her hair, as if Asian hair needed straightening. Then she folded waves into it with the straightener. It was the first time someone had managed to get curls to stay in her hair, aside from using copious amounts of hairspray and pinching curlers. Bri watched the whole palaver in the mirror, repeatedly reminding herself she was an officer of the law, an inspector with the SFPD and this was for the greater good—although she couldn't quite see it at that moment.

"Done!"

Kirsty spun the chair, and Hayes came over. "Wow. Who knew you were a girl?"

Bri scowled, but on the whole, she really liked the way her hair fell around her shoulders in silky waves. "What was the other stuff?"

"Come to the back."

An hour later, Bri was sorry she had asked. Emerging from the room, her legs, underarms, and bikini line tingled painfully. Hayes averted her eyes. "Why was that necessary?" Her teeth gritted.

"Uh, I just thought…while I had a hold of you…"

"You mean…this was your doing?! I could have just shaved, you know."

"Well…" Hayes shrugged apologetically. "Come on.

I'll buy you lunch to make up for it."

"It'll take more than lunch to make up for *that*."

24
LINA

I hate parties. So many men, each with expectations and desires. I have to say though, they are more likely to behave en masse. I stand in a corner with two other girls from my room. We have been cleaned and primped by Big Woman, whose name I now know to be Sasha. It is strange to know what she is called after a year in this hell. A year…has it really been that long? How have I endured all this abuse?

After I left Mr. Korschev's office, I lay in bed considering my time in these circumstances. Shame flooded my body. I was an object, used and cast aside.

Little Lina, let me help. Let me come out to play…

I jam my hands on either side of my head. The voice has become more prevalent since Max left. He kept me sane—am I going mad? No, it's simply not possible. I am intelligent. I can keep myself together.

One of the girls next to me nudges my arm. We are being approached by a pair of suited men. I try to focus through the haze of alcohol. We have been plied liberally with drink. It makes us more amenable, they say. Before I came here, I never drank much. Now, I relish the numbing effects of alcohol. Instinctively, I straighten my skirt, if it can be called that.

One man is almost handsome; the other is repulsive. I pray I get a bit of luck, for once. It would be nice to have something good happen… I laugh inside. Have I been reduced to finding happiness in the oddest of things? I smile, trying to look appealing. The handsome man takes my hand, leading me to a back bedroom…

*** * ***

I wish I had been chosen by the fat man now. The handsome man is only nice on the surface. The bruises will heal over time, but my soul is damaged beyond repair.

Come on, Lina. Let me out. I'll make it better, I promise.

The voice is harsher now; raspy, demanding. I almost give in.

I can protect you. You won't feel a thing. I'll make sure of it.

My throat still stings from the handsome man's hands. "No…"

You know you want to… Come on, Little Lina… Let me out to play…

25

"Holy shit." Trent's eyes bugged out of his head as Bri returned to the precinct. He grabbed Hayes' arm. "What have you done with my partner? Do I need to put out an APB?"

"No All-Points Bulletin necessary, Trent. I've just polished her up a bit."

"Would you two stop talking about me like I'm not here? It's really annoying."

The little black dress, as Hayes called it, fit Bri like a second skin. It stopped mid-thigh, and Bri was actually grateful Hayes had subjected her to a leg wax. In fact, there was something wonderful about not nicking herself with the razor while she balanced in the shower. The dress exposed one shoulder, with the other covered in a sheer layer, and a cutout neckline which revealed just a hint of her collarbone. It wasn't ostentatious, and Bri was grateful for Kastner's adherence to style and taste. She did find it unusual that he had such an ability, but the man had been full of surprises since they had met, so it wasn't too farfetched.

Kastner met them in the lobby wearing a tailored black suit with a dark red shirt and black tie. His hair had been combed and parted to the side with gel.

Hayes clasped her hands together. "It's like they're going to prom!"

Bri sighed. "This is an undercover operation, Cat. We have to take it seriously."

Kastner nodded his agreement, lifting his suit jacket to reveal the shoulder holster. "Yes, and since you can't go armed, I'll cover both of us, should something happen." He dropped the jacket. "Now, the van will be opposite the restaurant, but I've arranged a town car for us."

"What's our cover?" Bri forgot about her attire and was all business again.

"Every Monday night, Sokolov hosts a vodka tasting evening for some of his elite clientele…"

"How many types of vodka can there be?" Bri interrupted.

Kastner laughed. "Enough, Inspector… Oh. Maybe we should give you a cover name."

Trent lifted a finger. "Barbie." Bri shot out a fist, nailing him hard in the upper arm. "Ouch! Hey, you said it before, not me!"

"No, it needs to fit her…cover. You don't speak Korean, do you?"

Bri crossed her arms. "No, I don't."

"I think…for all intents and purposes, you should remain quiet by my side. Only speak in whispers to me and if anyone else addresses you, just lower your eyes demurely. You can be demure, can't you, Inspector?"

"I think you're all enjoying this *way* too much."

"Anyway, a name… Min. Yes, your name will be Min. And in reference to me, you will always call me 'sir.'"

Bri balked and her temper started to flare at the obvious submissive nature he was wanting her to portray. Then she remembered Lina and calmed down. "And what if someone there happens to speak Korean?"

Kastner smiled. "The same goes. I doubt anyone would be foolish enough to directly address you anyway."

"Why is that?"

"The men at these parties know when a woman is…" He coughed, reddening. "…under…ownership…"

Bri bristled, ready to burst out her objections, but she recognized that Kastner was only using the quickest means to get information. Besides, if no one was speaking to her, she would have a better chance to observe and listen to those around her. "Right."

"On that note, we should get miked up…although I don't know where they are going to put yours." Kastner made another joke, and Bri wondered if he was warming to them. Or, maybe, he was just getting into character. It was hard to tell.

Trent gestured to a room off reception. "In here, folks."

Hayes tugged Bri aside and gave her a tight hug. "Be careful. I know you always are, but…yeah, these guys are scum. Just…don't get alone with any of them."

Bri pressed her cheek to Hayes'. "Don't worry, Cat. This is my job. I know what I'm doing."

* * *

The town car slid up to the Little Russian Tea Room, and the driver opened the door for Kastner and Bri. Portraying the consummate gentleman, Kastner offered Bri his hand to assist her out of the car. She nearly forgot her role and was about to give him a tongue lashing, but checked herself in time, as she noticed they were being closely observed by a few couples entering the establishment.

Kastner tugged her arm through his, whispering, "Relax. You look as stiff as a board."

Bri hissed back, "This isn't exactly how I usually work an investigation." She did her best to plaster a placid smile on her reddened lips, lowering her eyes as they entered the establishment, the doorman taking her black wool coat, another unexpected addition provided by Kastner.

"Just watch. I'll do the rest."

Bri knew their words would be picked up in the van across the street, where Trent sat, along with two other officers who been recruited for the operation. "I hope you know what you're doing…" Before she could say more, Sokolov—Bri recognized him from the photograph—clocked them.

"Ah, my friend! How are you?" He shook Kastner's hand, but there was something unnatural about how his face paled subtly and his eyes darted about, then up and down Bri. "And who is your lovely guest this evening?"

"Her name is Min. A recent acquisition to my collection."

Collection? Bri inwardly groaned, but kept her expression neutral, eyes down.

Sokolov lifted her hand in a practiced motion and placed a dry kiss on the back. "A pleasure. I hope you will enjoy your evening?" He intentionally tried to catch Bri's eyes, but she kept them fixed on a spot on the floor, just in front of his highly polished shoes.

"She doesn't speak much English, I'm afraid. We have other means of communicating, if you know what I mean." Out of the corner of her eye, Bri caught Kastner making a lewd wink. Is this what those girls were being subjected to? She imagined Kastner was well-practiced in the methods and behaviors of these traffickers.

"Ah! I understand completely. Please, have this table by the window. The service will begin shortly."

Bri was familiar with Russian cuisine—thanks to her mother's side of the family—but she was under the impression this would only be a tasting session. However, her stomach grumbled, since she hadn't eaten anything since the hasty lunch with Hayes earlier in the day, although part of the upset she attributed to the unexpected nerves she felt. Or was it something other than nerves? Maybe anticipation?

Kastner nudged her, motioning to the seat being held out by the smartly dressed maître-d'. Sokolov obviously spared no expense at his gatherings. She sat, allowing the chair to be pushed in under her. She desperately wanted to ask Kastner questions, but he simply sat, pulling her hand into his and stroking his thumb over the palm. His eyes met hers and she read him as clear as if he had spoken—we're playing a role. Start acting like it.

Bri threw caution to the wind and placing a hand over her mouth, she gave her best emulation of a giggle. The unexpected sound amused Kastner as he gave her hand a tug, forcing her to lean in. He spoke through smiling teeth. "The man who just came in is Andrei Korschev. He is on our list of known traffickers...we just don't have any evidence."

Subtly swiveling her head, she caught sight of the large man in a well-fitting suit. None of the buttons strained, nor did the waistband of the trousers look stretched. It was tailor-made to fit his rotund form. On his arm was a slim, sickly-looking woman with straight, blonde hair and rounded eyes. She was wearing a dark blue dress, much the same style as hers, except this woman's exposed an ample amount of cleavage. She had been adorned with what Bri could only assume were real diamonds on her ears, wrist, and neck.

Kastner's squeeze of her hand drew her attention back as a young waitress served the first course, *borscht*, a beet and cabbage soup Bri had seen her grandfather consume on many an occasion. Thankfully, this one was warm, as opposed to the usual cold way her grandfather ate it. As she tried to delicately consume the soup, she constantly observed the room, noticing the majority of the couples were older men with younger, prettier women. She filed away her questions for after the operation was complete.

The appetizer was followed by beef stroganoff on egg noodles. Bri ate sparingly after noticing a lot of the women only had one or two bites. She thought it would do her well to copy them, in order not to draw suspicion. Kastner's subtle nod gave her the approval she needed to continue the act. While Bri was nibbling on a Russian tea cake, not really a tea cake at all, but more a butter cookie with walnuts and covered in powdered sugar, Sokolov drew the guests' attention to him. Bri played ignorant, pretending she had only looked up because Kastner had.

"I am pleased you all have come to join me tonight. This evening, we will present six vodkas to taste. If you choose, there are other refreshments available in the back." The meaning was clear. Anyone wanting something stronger than vodka would find it there.

Bri had never been to a vodka tasting, or any type of tasting, before. The closest she usually got to alcohol was her beer and wine sessions with Hayes and Trent. She'd have to follow Kastner's lead.

"As you know, the best way—the Russian way—to taste vodka appropriately is to have it frozen." As he spoke, waiters began to distribute frost-clouded glasses to each of the patrons, serving them on polished silver trays. A measure of vodka was placed in each.

"I only speak for the new ones amongst us." Sokolov's chuckles were echoed by the other, more seasoned guests, including Korschev. "Now, warm the glass only slightly in your hands…"

Bri made out she was mimicking Kastner, who gestured to her.

"There are three things we must consider: smell, sight, and taste. Vodka, my friends, is not just a base for other drinks. Swirl it in your glass and smell. You will see this one does not smell like your cheap shit." The sudden profanity resulted in more laughter. "Now, see how the liquid is clouded. I think this one has a bluish tint. There is an energy about it…"

It was an art form to Sokolov, Bri thought. But still, she couldn't dismiss the way these men enjoyed all this finery and still abused women so openly. She thought of Max, murdered and disposed of as if he was a dirty Kleenex.

"Now, we taste. Let it roll over your palate. See how smooth it is, how creamy, how soft…like a good woman, eh?" More laughter. "Now, swallow."

The guests all complied, and murmurs of assent rose up amongst the group.

"That, my friends, was a Stoli Elit: Himalayan Edition, produced by Stolichnaya. It retails at $3,000 a bottle. Why is it so expensive? Well, it uses the purest waters from the Himalayan Mountains, mixed with Russian winter wheat."

The procedure was repeated six times, and by the end, Bri was grateful for the heavy meal prior to the tasting. Out of the corner of her eye, she saw Korschev approach Sokolov as the guests started to mingle. She made a few gestures to Kastner, signifying that she needed the bathroom. His brow pinched, but he nodded, knowing she would pass the pair on the way.

As she gingerly crossed the restaurant, Bri developed the uncomfortable sensation that every man in the room was watching her—it wasn't ego, it was a simple fact, only exemplified by her own research on how Russian men desired Asian women. According to Hayes, her features were unique, which would lead some men to question her ethnic background. She supposed Kastner would explain that away easily enough, if questioned.

She rounded the corner toward the restroom, stopping just out of sight of Korschev and Sokolov.

"Is everything prepared?"

"Yes, yes, but you know I don't enjoy speaking like this while I have guests."

"Vasily, I am not a patient man. It is enough that I have given you some leeway in this endeavor. Do not ask me to make further concessions!" Korschev's voice was low, threatening.

"You can count on me. I have a room prepared."

"And it is secured from the outside?"

"Yes! It is all arranged." Bri could imagine Sokolov wiping sweat from his brow.

"Now, your niece...I should like to take her to dinner..."

Bri chose that moment to pretend to emerge from the bathroom and began making a beeline for her table with Kastner, when a hand wrapped around her upper arm, not forcefully, but enough to restrain.

"What have we here? An Oriental bloom in your restaurant, Sokolov? Where have you been hiding her?"

"I...I...she..." Sokolov fumbled for an answer while Bri resisted the urge to rip her arm from Korschev's grasp.

"She belongs to me." Kastner was at her side, extracting her arm, and possessively cupping a hand around her waist. Bri's heart rate sped up as she looked down and away, wanting nothing more than to knee Korschev in the groin.

"And who are you? I don't remember seeing you here before."

There was a harshness to Kastner's voice which Bri hadn't noticed before, an accent, maybe? German?

"Yes, we are visiting. Sokolov was kind enough to host us, but I believe we should be going."

"How much for her? Five thousand?" Korschev eyed Bri lecherously.

"She is not for sale." Kastner bowed his head to Sokolov. "Thank you for another wonderful evening. I will be back to talk business when you are free." He unceremoniously escorted Bri out the door.

26

Bri took off her heels as soon as they entered the town car. They would debrief with the rest of the team in the morning to prevent breaking cover. "If my mic caught all the conversation, your informant—the one who doesn't participate *at all* in trafficking—is planning on holding one of Korschev's girls there."

Kastner silently stared at the back of the head of their driver, an officer from Central. His expression was troubled. "We need more evidence. I'll have to listen to the tapes before I order any type of raid on the premises."

"What? You need more evidence? What more could you need? That girl could help us locate Lina…"

"Inspector, it's a shot in the dark, and you know it. The fact of the matter is, we don't know where Lina is. She could be in another state by now!" Kastner shifted to face her. "There comes a point where we might have to accept defeat."

Bri knew he was right, but some part of her was unwilling to. "Have you ever heard of following your gut, Kastner?"

"Yes, but…"

"That's what I'm doing. I can't explain it, but I have a

feeling all this is leading us somewhere. I don't want Max to have died in vain." Bri shoved her hair off her face. "Damn, I don't know how some women do this every day. I want to scrub my face, get into sweats and veg out with a beer in front of the TV." She sighed. "All those women in there…"

Kastner nodded. "Probably about eighty percent of them, I would guess. Korschev runs a lucrative escort service."

"I wish I could have spoken to one of them. Maybe I could have gotten some information, any information."

"Unlikely. Opening your mouth often means punishment, or, as you saw with the girl in the morgue, death. If she had gone quietly, there is a likelihood she would still be alive."

"That's pretty crass, Kastner."

"I know. You know what? We're not so different. I want these things too, Bri…Inspector Ryu." He wrung his hands. "Maybe something will turn up in trace. Your medical examiner did a thorough autopsy and evidence collection?"

"Hayes is the best. She doesn't miss a thing." Bri crossed her arms and wiggled her toes. "That's so much better."

"You did look really nice, Inspector." Kastner attempted a smile.

"Are you hitting on me, Agent?"

Kastner flushed. "No…you're not my type."

Bri leaned back in the seat, all fight flickering out like a candle. "I can't wait to get home."

"I'll have the driver drop you off. No point in going back to the station tonight."

"Yeah, thanks. Hey, how did you get involved in the Anti-Trafficking Task Force anyway? You never said." It was a simple question, however, by the way Kastner sighed and melted into the seat next to her, she

121

understood it might not be answered in the same way.

"My great-uncle was Rudolf Kastner. Do you know who he is?"

Bri shook her head, giving him her undivided attention.

"He was a lawyer. During World War II, he was involved with attempts to rescue people sent to concentration camps. However, there was a great deal of controversy surrounding his actual efforts and, in the end, he was assassinated. When I found out about this piece of family history, I decided I wanted to do something where there was little doubt as to my motivations. I wanted to help people who had been brought to this country under force. It became an obsession, trying to get women out from under these traffickers." He stared out the tinted window as the lights from the city dimmed. For a few moments, the only sounds were the rush of cars around them and the whir of their own car's engine as it hummed along the freeway.

"I sense a 'but'..." Bri murmured softly.

"Yes, but I became too close to the situation once and had to take a step back. I relocated to the west coast and began advising the task force here."

"Too close?" Bri knew she was prying, something she didn't like to do, but curiosity had gotten the better of her.

"One girl. We pulled her out from a raid on a massage parlor in New York. We arranged everything—T-visa, shelter, therapy—but in the end, she went back, informed the traffickers of what we were planning in regards to other raids, and they had the opportunity to move the women before we got to them. My own stupidity, my own misguided desire to gain her trust, ruined months of investigation and surveillance."

She watched his fingers curl into a fist, the knuckles going white against his flesh. Placing a hand over his, she watched him twitch, then his eyes shifted to hers. "I feel the same about Max. I wonder if I could have made sure he couldn't have run away...done something to gain his trust faster..."

"He did trust you, Inspector. He came to you. I don't think he would have, had he not thought you would believe him."

"How could he know that?"

"Anything, really. A newspaper article, perhaps? Did anything memorable happen prior to that?" Kastner seemed relieved that the topic had shifted away from his past experiences.

"Well...It's hard to recall..." Bri lifted her hand away from his. "There was this one thing...at a local school. I went to talk to the kids and a reporter from the SF Chronicle got wind of it. He came to take a picture of us. We were talking about how to be safe, not to talk to people they don't know, have a password with their parents so they know if someone other than them is coming to pick them up...that sort of stuff."

"Then that's it, Inspector. He must have seen the story."

"Maybe. It doesn't sit well with me that we'll never know. Do you think he told his sister?"

"We're speculating now?" He gave her a half-smile. "No, I understand. It's hard to live in a world of facts and statistics. Sometimes, we need to try to see a bigger picture. Let's see, if I was Max, I probably wouldn't have told my sister. I would probably feel an obligation to get her out of the situation she was in. Maybe, though, I was too young to fully understand the circumstances, but I'd been forced to grow up faster than I had to."

Bri worried her lip between her teeth. "Yeah...I worry we're not going to make it in time."

"Let's see what happens in the next few days. Trace and the stomach contents should be back, and we can cross our fingers that something comes up." Kastner patted her arm as the car stopped in front of her apartment complex. "Until tomorrow, Inspector. Try to get some sleep."

Smiling back at him, she waited for the driver to open her door. "Kastner?"

"Yeah?"

"You're a good one. I'm sorry I judged you before."

The smile was easily returned. "Think nothing of it. First impressions aren't my forte."

Bri nodded and shut the door. He was right. Trace was coming back, and a niggling feeling in her gut told her this would bring the break they were hoping for.

27
LINA

I am woken in the middle of the night again by Sasha, the Big Woman. My brain has blotted out all the aches and pains until I am a walking shell. I feel nothing. I am numb to it all.

"Come on. He's waiting." She curls her hand around my upper arm, encircling it easily. I am skin and bones.

Liiiiinnnnaaaaa! Kick her. I can do it for you…

"No!" My voice is hoarse with sleep.

"Excuse me?" Her eyes are cold, unfeeling. Her grip tightens, like she wants to snap my bones.

"I…am sorry. My legs…are…" I straighten and clear my throat. "I am coming."

"Good girl. No use trying to rebel now. You know what will happen, *kotyonok*."

My mind pores over my knowledge of Russian. Kitten. She has called me kitten. Like a beloved pet. I am a pet, only not so beloved.

She raps her knuckles on the door. "*Ser*, I have the girl."

"Enter," Korschev's rough voice comes from the

other side.

She opens the door and shoves me in, shutting it behind me. I am alone.

Not alone, Little Lina.

I wince, closing my eyes tightly. Where is this voice coming from? Who is she…he?

No, it most certainly doesn't sound like a 'she.'

Korschev's face softens, if that is even possible, as his steely eyes inspect my trembling form. "Come here, Lina." He rolls back the chair and pats his lap.

An acidic taste creeps into the base of my throat, and I swallow hard, willing myself not to throw up on his polished shoes. I unconsciously move my legs, robotic, as I comply with his request. His hands span my narrow waist.

"Lina…my dear…you have been so obedient. There are hardly any complaints about you. You make my life easy," Korschev coos as he trails fat fingers up and down my bare arm. I repress the urge to shudder.

I know what is expected as he pauses. "Thank you, sir."

"I would like to move you to a new house…a better one. Would you like that, *malishka*?"

Baby. I am not his baby. Leon called me that…

His grip on my waist tightens, and I remember where I am.

"Yes, sir. Thank you, sir."

Fingers are probing between my thighs now.

"Of course, I should make sure you're as pliable as I think." He hurls me forward over the desk, knocking the wind out of me. His hand fists painfully in my hair, and I bite my lip to stifle a scream. As he presses my face into the papered surface, the door opens, and a man I recognize walks in.

"Hello, Lina *malishka*."

Leon.

28

Bri latched her hands on either side of the white porcelain sink, staring at her reflection in the misted-over bathroom mirror. All traces of make-up and hairspray had been washed away and she was beginning to feel much more like herself. As she breathed in the steam in a steady rhythm, she thought of the women at the party last night. They had been all smiles and giggles, but the eyes…their eyes remained dead.

Two faces, she thought. They show two faces to the world.

A revelation dawned on her with such force, her knees nearly caved. There had been times when they'd had to work with prostitutes who had been raped. Usually, there were special inspectors on call for that type of crime, but if they were short-handed, Bri and Trent sometimes handled the calls. She thought of the reporters, the media, who would ignore any sex crime involving a pro. If she remembered rightly, one of them had said, 'Sometimes, the women choose to do this.'

Bri ripped the towel off her head, ruffling her hair viciously. No one chose this. No matter what anyone said, it was a damned perception that the women had a choice.

She grumbled at her outburst of temper, knowing she would have tangled her fine hair into knots. Leaving the bathroom, she sought out a comb, nearly screaming as she searched for where she had left the damned thing.

As she teased the tangles from the ends of her hair, Bri sat on her bed. Her cell phone screen on the nightstand remained blank. After the op, Meyers had insisted she come in late. The FBI would be doing some untangling of their own, analyzing the tapes recorded from the previous night. She hoped they'd yield some clues to what this Korschev was doing…maybe when they were speaking Russian…

Her cell vibrated to life and she snatched it, comb still knotted in her hair. "This is Ryu."

"Inspector Ryu…it's Petra." The voice sounded shaky, uncertain.

"Ms. Vasquez…Petra…what's the matter?" Bri straightened on the bed.

"It's Nadia, Inspector. She's gone."

* * *

Bri's hand slammed into the door leading to the Investigations Department. She narrowed her eyes, scanning the room, catching sight of Trent by the coffee machine. Crossing to him, she grabbed his arm.

"Hey, you."

Any other time, she would have retorted at the quip about her last name, but there was only one thing she was focused on. "Trent, Nadia is missing."

"Nadia…?"

"The girl from the shelter. Petra…Ms. Vasquez called me. I rushed in." Her breath came in heaved gasps.

"Whoa, whoa. Calm down, Bri." He landed a comforting hand on her shoulder. "Come on. We'll go see her. Call her, okay?" His eyes skimmed over Bri's panicked face. "Maybe it's nothing. It's a big city…"

"That's what I'm afraid of. In a big city, anyone can get lost."

"Who's lost?" Meyers' smooth voice interrupted their conversation, and Bri turned to face him, Trent's hand slipping from her shoulder.

"A witness, Captain. We need to go interview the woman who brought her to us." Bri bit the inside of her cheek, waiting for the customary time-wasting response.

Meyers appeared to contemplate what she was saying for the length of time it would take a sloth to cross a tree branch. "Go on. I have a meeting with Agent Kastner to debrief on last night's operation. He assures me it was a success. We can't lose our stride now."

Bri didn't hesitate. She began to dial Petra's number on her cell. "Thanks, Cap." She lifted the phone to her ear, as Trent grabbed his jacket and followed her out of the building to the street below.

When Petra picked up, Bri could tell she was quite shaken. "Inspector."

"We need to meet, Petra." Bri dispatched with the formalities. "Where?"

Petra rattled off the name of a Starbucks, the same one they had met at before. Bri nodded. "See you there." She hung up, relaying the conversation to Trent.

"Okay, okay…" He stopped her, turning her to face him, hands on both shoulders. "Briana, breathe!"

His soft brown gaze peered down at what she knew would be her reddening face. The tears began to sting, and she cursed her weakness.

"Bri, you're getting too close to this case. I know we all do from time to time, but unless you snap back into the objective inspector I know and love, we're not going to be able to find Lina."

Pedestrians pushed past them, some of them grumbling at the obstruction they were creating on the sidewalk. Trent remained oblivious.

Focusing on his concerned face, Bri's chin dropped. "I know."

"It's…your grandfather again, isn't it?" The usual I-told-you-so didn't precede his question. They both knew she'd thrown herself back into work too early, and if she didn't gain some perspective fast, she would make a mistake.

"I need work, Billy. I need this. I need to do…something. Max came to me for help…and I didn't make it in time." The tears did fall at this point.

Trent cupped her chin in his hand, lifting her dampening face. "You are Briana Ryu. I've seen you take down guys twice your size, but you are not invincible."

"I have to help her."

"You're not in control of this and that scares you. You weren't in control when pulmonary fibrosis took your grandpa, either."

Memories of the previous months came flooding back, nearly crushing her chest with the emotional force. When she had received the call from her mom, Bri had collapsed to the floor, the sobs coming in huge heaves.

"These men…they don't care about the women they take. Nadia escaped that, but I have this…fear she has been taken again. Can we please just do this? I'll…talk about it later, I promise. You and Cat can come over tonight. Okay?"

Trent knew her well enough to know when she needed to talk and when she needed to carry on, as if everything was normal. This was a normal moment, so he nodded and released her with a gentle squeeze of her shoulders, and they continued to their destination.

* * *

When they finally arrived at the Starbucks, Petra wasn't hard to spot. She sat at a corner table, her eyes shifting frantically back and forth as she picked at her cuticles. Bri knew she would be experiencing a high level of stress due to Nadia going missing, but she didn't expect this normally composed and strong woman to look so beaten.

"Get us some coffee, Trent, please." Bri inclined her head to the line at the counter. Trent was about to object, but then he clocked Petra as well. His mouth closed, and he nodded, his expression turning serious.

Bri proceeded to the table, making sure not to creep up on Petra. She thought if she did, the poor woman would most likely scream. "Petra?" she murmured softly, hoping her calm exterior would soothe the agitated women.

Petra's head shot up, and she gave Bri a shaky smile. "Inspector…I'm so relieved to see you."

Bri sat opposite her. "What happened?"

"I was doing my normal bed checks and hers was empty, not even slept in. So, I looked at the sign-in sheet for the shelter and she had left around eleven that morning. She was meeting with a tutor for her studies, but she never came back."

"Does she have a cell phone?" Bri couldn't help reaching across and placing a hand over the other woman's trembling ones.

"Yes…but when we tried it, she didn't answer. Then, after a few hours, it went straight to voicemail instead."

"Have you slept?"

Petra shook her head. "No…no…" Her voice turned hoarse and the tears began to trickle down her paling cheeks, a shade lighter than her normal skin tone.

"If you give me her cell phone number, I'll see if we can get notified if it gets turned on again."

Petra rattled off a number, and Bri quickly wrote it down on a napkin. She took out her own phone and dialed the IT unit.

"Kevin? It's Inspector Ryu."

"Hey, Inspector, what can I do for you?"

She heard the crinkle of a candy wrapper and rolled her eyes. "I need a trace on a cell phone, and if it's currently turned off, I want to be notified ASAP if it bounces off any towers."

"Gotcha. Fire when ready."

Bri repeated the number slowly, and Freedman parroted it back. She heard the tapping of keys.

"Gimme about thirty seconds to see if it's on…"

The line went silent. Bri leaned forward on the table as Trent returned with their coffee. The seconds ticked by as tension rose between the trio. Finally, after what seemed like an eternity, Freedman's voice came back on the line.

"I'm really sorry, Inspector, but the phone is either switched off or dead. I'll leave the program running and call you the minute I get a ping." He hung up.

"Damn it." Bri pocketed her cell phone. "We get to play the waiting game. In the meantime, I'd like to go talk to her tutor. We can get a timeline going of where she's been."

"I did call the tutor." Petra regained her composure. "He said she left about one, as usual."

"Did he ask where she was going?"

"No, he assumed she was returning to the shelter."

Bri took a much-needed slurp of coffee, feeling the caffeine pulse through her. "We need to take a walk, Petra. I know you don't want to tell us where your shelter is, and I completely understand that, but it is imperative we figure out the route she might have taken. Also, if she passed any stores…maybe even homeless people. Someone might have seen her. Do you have a picture?"

Reaching into her jacket, Petra retrieved a photograph of a stern-looking Nadia. "It's from her visa photo."

Bri handed it over to Trent. "Okay, time to do some legwork." Snatching a final sip of coffee, the two inspectors pushed back their chairs.

Petra stood up. "I'm coming with you."
"I was counting on it."

29

Petra escorted them from the coffee shop, taking a right, then a left. After a few blocks, Bri began to recognize the pattern. She was deliberately altering her path, in case someone was following her. She took the most populated roads, even if it meant adding time to her journey. Bri caught her arm.

"Would Nadia have done what you're doing now?"

Petra nodded. "Yes, we teach all our girls that there is safety by not taking shortcuts."

Trent's cell rang and he picked it up, dropping back behind them, making little response as the person on the other end of the phone spoke. Bri glanced over her shoulder and spotted him nodding a few times. Finally, he hung up and strode to Bri's side.

"Kastner. He said trace is back on Max's body. We need to meet him at the medical examiner's office when we're done here."

"That's fine."

Petra stopped in front of a tall building. "This is where the tutor works." They entered and approached the reception desk—an elaborate wooden and marble structure—where an overweight security guard sat, doing a crossword puzzle.

Bri and Trent flashed their IDs and the man straightened in his seat. "How can I help you, Inspectors?"

"We're wondering if you saw this girl leave here…about one yesterday afternoon. Were you on shift?"

The man bobbed his head in the affirmative. "Yes, yes, I remember her. She comes here about three times a week. Always says hi and bye."

"Did you see anyone go after her? Maybe someone speaking to her?" Trent leaned on the marble countertop.

"No, she said bye and left, like she usually does. She smiled too…" He hung his head. "I went back to my puzzle. I'm sorry. Is she okay?"

"If you remember anything, please call us." Bri slid her card over to him, not willing to give away anything about Nadia she didn't have to. Petra stood stiffly next to her. "Thank you for your time." She took Petra's arm and guided her out, as Trent followed.

"Okay, where from here, Ms. Vasquez?" Trent glanced up and down the street.

"Uh, right." Petra hesitated.

"What's the matter?"

"He's…there's something obvious about your partner's presence, Inspector Ryu."

Bri sighed. It was true Trent sometimes stuck out like a sore thumb with his good looks and tall stature. "Look, Trent, why don't you go back to the station and check on Freedman's progress? I'll be back in about an hour."

Trent didn't look much like he wanted to leave his partner. "You sure?"

"Yeah, two women are less conspicuous." Bri smiled at him. "Besides, we're just on a walk."

Trent sighed. "Okay. Call me as soon as you're headed back." With a final glance over the two women, he reluctantly departed, hands in his pockets.

Turning to Petra, Bri touched her arm. "Let's go."

The walk resumed in silence until Petra spoke up. "Do you struggle, Inspector?"

Lines creased between Bri's brows as she lifted her eyes to Petra. "I'm sorry?"

"Being…as you are."

Something inside Bri braced itself for action. This was the type of wording she typically heard when people asked about her preference in partners—and not the working kind. She was usually pretty open about her sexuality—assuming that's what Petra was referring to. Or she might be referencing her role as an inspector. Bri's head searched for the right answer, but, as a good investigator, she knew further information was needed.

"I'm sorry, I don't know what you mean…?" She left the question open, hoping Petra would fill in the blanks.

Petra's lower lip caught between her teeth. "I mean…you…like women, right?"

The tone didn't imply any type of disdain. It was an entirely honest question, but her extended silence as she grappled with the decision to reveal any intimate details of her life must have caused Petra to sense discomfort.

"I'm sorry. That was quite forward of me."

Bri's thoughts rebounded around her brain, and finally triggered her mouth to issue forth words. "Yeah, I do. I also like men." What the hell had made her confide this to a virtual stranger, and even worse, one who was part of an active investigation? Bri recalled her earlier attraction to the woman beside her and wondered if she was losing some semblance of common sense.

"Oh I…just find it hard, so I was wondering if you experienced similar things? I mean, I know we do live in a very liberal area, but some might say my preferences are because of my situation with the traffickers…that I hate men."

Bri sighed. This was a discussion she had had with Hayes on a few occasions, how people thought events in a person's life shaped their sexual preference. "No, I don't think that way. I'm kinda under the belief we are born the way we are and there's nothing wrong with that."

"And your family?"

Bri knew she was lucky. Her entire family had been supportive. It wasn't the norm. She knew people often were disowned by their families, forced to fend for themselves, some even turning to illicit and illegal activities to survive. Still, she was glad social perceptions were changing.

"My family has been great."

Petra turned another corner, the people walking around them thinning out. "I do not think my parents would have approved. They are dead now. I haven't had the…courage to seek out any of my extended family since…"

"I think we do things when we are ready. That's all that matters." Bri shifted the conversation topic, trying not to let her libido take over. It had been a while since she'd been in any kind of meaningful relationship. Her job was her life, but there was still that niggle, that desire to come home to someone who would understand about her work. *Maybe Petra…no. Don't be stupid, woman!*

"Inspector!" Petra shouted out, stopping before a small opening between two buildings.

Bri jogged up, scanning the dimly lit alcove. Her eyes landed on a pair of pink Converse sticking from under trash bags. "Shit, shit…" She stayed Petra with a hand on the shoulder. "Call Trent and stay here. Give him our location."

She handed Petra her cell phone before unholstering her SIG Sauer duty weapon. Keeping her right finger in line with the trigger guard, she stepped forward, firearm at the ready. Once completely satisfied that there was no one lurking in any corners or behind the dumpster, she holstered her weapon. The sound of sirens began to fade in from the distance.

Bri approached the sneakers, clearly attached to a pair of jeans-encased legs. She shifted the bags and the battered face of Nadia came into view. Quickly assessing her, Bri noticed Nadia's clothing didn't look disturbed, but that didn't mean she hadn't been sexually assaulted. Cautiously pressing index and middle fingers to her carotid artery, Bri held her breath. A strong pulse. She exhaled and remained kneeling by Nadia's side.

"She has a pulse," she called out to Petra, who looked on the verge of collapse.

"Oh, thank God. Thank God!"

At that moment, Trent came rushing to the scene. "Oh, shit. Bri…"

"She's alive. Condition unknown. Paramedics en route?"

"Yeah, yeah…" His hand went to the grip of his weapon, but Bri shook her head.

"There's no one here."

"Right. I'll direct the cavalry."

Within minutes, paramedics were bustling into the alleyway, their priority to get the injured woman to a hospital. Bri grumbled at the possible loss of forensic evidence, but with Nadia alive, she would be their best chance of finding out what had happened. Trent guided Petra aside, speaking in hushed tones as the woman watched the paramedics load Nadia onto a gurney.

"I want to go with her," Bri overheard her saying.

"No, Inspector Ryu will. If Nadia regains consciousness, it's important we get a clear statement." Trent's voice was reassuring. He had a mode he entered when dealing with traumatized people. It was his forte, actually. That imposing presence made people feel safe in those moments.

Bri followed the gurney, trying to smile at Petra. "They're taking her to St. Francis ER. Trent'll drive you."

Petra pressed a hand to her mouth, as she caught a full glimpse of Nadia's battered face. Trent quickly guided her away into the back of a patrol car, as Bri hoisted herself into the ambulance. She wanted answers, and at this point, she wasn't willing to let anyone stop her.

※ ※ ※

Upon arrival at St. Francis, one of the only not-for-profit hospitals in the city—and also the closest to the scene of the assault—Bri was summarily removed from the treatment bay by a stern, but well-meaning, nurse. She sank into a hard plastic-covered chair outside the door, dropping her head into her hands. How much more trauma could one woman endure? Nadia had been through so much in her reasonably short life. She was trying to better herself, get an education, start a new life. What had happened when she left the tutoring center? Who knew where she was? Who had recognized her? Bri was so deep in thought with these questions, that she yelped when a hand landed on her shoulder.

"Sorry!" Hayes' eyes widened as she jumped back. "Yeesh."

"Cat…what are you doing here?"

"They called me in to take trace from…Nadia, was it?" She indicated to her kit. "What happened, Bri?" Kneeling by her chair, Hayes took Bri's hands in hers.

"We…"

The door to the treatment room swung open, and a tall man in scrubs was pulling gloves off his hands. "Are you the woman's guardian?"

Bri leapt up, almost knocking Hayes down in the process, who grumbled as she got to her feet. "She doesn't have a guardian…she's…a survivor of human trafficking." Bri felt the need to lower her voice as some means of keeping Nadia safe should anyone be watching or listening.

"Ah, I see. And you are…?"

"Inspector Briana Ryu," Bri flashed her ID badge, "and this is Dr. Catriona Hayes, the medical examiner."

"Dr. Laine." He crumpled the gloves in his hand. "We need a name for the record…" He pulled a file out of the holder by the door.

Bri shared a look with Hayes, who answered the doctor's question with full professionalism. "I think, based on the circumstances, Dr. Laine, we should refer to her as Jane Doe. Don't you agree?" Hayes' tone was firm, one which wouldn't allow for any refusal on the part of the other doctor.

Dr. Laine met Bri's eyes and she nodded in agreement. "Very well. Jane Doe. We will issue her with a number as well. I'll have the nurse apprise you of it when it's done."

"What's her condition?" Bri was eager to relay any news she could to Petra.

Dr. Laine cleared his throat. "Severe trauma to the face and nose. We want to do a CAT scan to rule out any internal injury to the brain."

Hayes picked up her kit. "I'd like to do my examination now, before evidence is lost."

"We figured that, so we will leave the rape kit to you."

"Do you think she was raped?" Bri couldn't conceal the panic rising in her voice. Hayes steadied her with a reassuring pat on the shoulder.

"Upon initial observation, no, but I'll leave that to your examiner to decide for certain."

Hayes angled her body to Bri. "Why don't you go see Trent and Ms. Vasquez? I'll do my examination and report back to you. I can also give you a rundown of the trace we found on the first victim." She began to follow

Dr. Laine. "Oh, and Bri?"

"Yeah?"

"Eat something."

Bri was finally able to snort with what could have been described as derision. "I…"

"It's nearly three in the afternoon. And I know you didn't have breakfast."

"Yes, *Mother*." Bri crossed her arms like a petulant child, as Hayes disappeared through the swinging doors.

30

Petra paced the waiting room; Inspector Trent was talking on the phone to someone she assumed must be a superior. Her eyes occasionally passed over the doorway, wondering when Inspector Ryu was coming back. She mentally cursed herself for asking about the inspector's personal life. She shouldn't pry. She was investigating the murder of this boy and trying to find his sister. Petra knew she should remain objective. Her priorities were her girls, Nadia especially. She had so much potential and then, this had to happen...this further traumatic experience to pound on her psyche.

It had been a long time since Petra had thought of her past. The time with the traffickers had felt like a nightmare—the ones where you try to run and find your legs won't move, no matter how much you will them to. It had been like a horror movie, and she recalled how disassociated she'd been from it all—as if she was floating above the entire experience—watching someone she didn't know go through the trauma.

Bri...Inspector Ryu, she reminded herself, was a competent woman. Petra had felt the budding attraction to her personality and fieriness, which is why she had agreed to help—if she could—in the first place. It had been a long time since she had even thought of her own emotions, her own desires. Still, it was a line she knew she could not cross, at least until they found out what had happened to Lina, poor girl.

Movement out of the corner of her eye had her revolving to face the door. Inspector Trent stood, crossing quickly to Inspector Ryu. "What's up?"

A man in scrubs followed closely behind her. "Hello, I'm Dr. Laine. I am told that one of you is the guardian for the young lady in my ER?"

Petra stepped forward immediately. "Yes, that's me, Petra Vasquez."

He nodded and smiled reassuringly. "I understand she was trafficked into the country and is essentially an emancipated minor?"

"Yes, yes, what's happened to her?"

"We believe she's experienced massive head trauma due to a physical assault. I'd like your permission to do a CAT scan on her to check for internal bleeding. She's stable for the moment, but I really want to rule out anything hidden." Dr. Laine had kind eyes, Petra thought, like the police officers who had found her when…

"Petra?" Inspector Ryu's gentle touch jolted her back to the present.

"Yes, yes, by all means. The charity has funds…"

Dr. Laine held up a hand. "St. Francis is a not-for-profit hospital, Ms. Vasquez. We will take care of Jane Doe to the best of our abilities."

"Jane…her name is…"

Inspector Trent had been speaking to Inspector Ryu but paused as he overheard and abruptly cut off Petra. "Yes…Jane Doe."

"I don't understand…"

"It's for safety purposes, Ms. Vasquez." The soft, warm pressure of Inspector Ryu's hand on her forearm dissipated her worries.

"Yes, of course. We must protect her..." She frantically scanned the other woman's eyes, searching for further reassurance as her anxiety spiked again.

The brown eyes were full of compassion. "Of course, Petra. We will make sure she is safe. Officers will be posted outside her room. I promise...nothing—and nobody—will touch her here, right Dr. Laine?"

"Yes, of course. We will place her on a secure ward. We are not unaccustomed to these circumstances here, I'm sad to say." A soft PA system sounded, repeating his name. "If you'll excuse me, I'll be in touch as soon as we know anything from the CAT scan. I believe your medical examiner should be finished soon as well." He nodded and departed.

"Examiner?" Petra's heart sped up again, as Inspector Ryu guided her to a chair, urging her to sit.

"We have to collect trace evidence and make sure Nadia was not...assaulted further."

Petra dragged her fingers through her hair, leaning forward, fighting the vomit burning her throat. "I...see..."

Trent cleared his throat. "I'll get more coffee." He left Petra alone with Inspector Ryu.

The soothing touch ran over her hair. "Petra...I'm so sorry."

Lifting her head, she met the eyes of the woman next to her. The exotic shaped orbs were brimming with unshed tears, a break in the carefully composed façade the inspector usually carried.

"Oh, Briana, please...I knew what I was doing..." On impulse, she grasped her hands and the roles reversed. Petra's desire to help those who were hurting overwhelmed her. "Nadia is alive because you took me seriously, because you listened."

A muscle flickered through Inspector Ryu's rounded

jawline, a feature which hinted at her Asian heritage. "I should have left you, and your girls, out of this…"

"But we must do all we can to help." Petra ran her thumbs over the other woman's palms. "Please, do not blame yourself. When Nadia wakes up, we can ask her what happened. She will tell us. She is strong, like you…"

"Like me? I don't think I'm the strong one here." A smile broke the distressed expression on Inspector Ryu's face. "I admire you, Petra. All you do, all you are… Maybe if circumstances were different…"

"They will be. Find Max's killer. Find his sister. Then…the future is open, isn't it?" Petra knew she was being bold, but she had quickly learned that to let important moments pass would lead to later regret, and she couldn't ignore the frisson of attraction she felt for Inspector Ryu.

"Yes…the future is always open."

Trent entered the room, and Petra released Inspector Ryu's hands on sight of his quirked eyebrow. "Bri, Nadia is awake."

31

Bri rubbed her palms, trying to stop them tingling. Had Petra really just admitted she found her attractive and wanted…more? She shook her head. No, for the moment, the focus had to be on the case, but isn't that what Petra had said as well? Trent kept casting sidelong glances at her as they walked down the corridor, following Petra's quick steps. She knew he wanted to ask about the scene he had encountered, but he would wait. If Trent was good at anything, it was biding his time until the appropriate moment.

The ward intercom buzzed as they identified themselves, coming face to face with a middle-aged nurse in hot pink scrubs as they entered the next room. Her top was covered in matching bright flowers which bloomed over her large chest. "Inspectors, Ms. Vasquez, please come this way. The young lady is asking for you."

When they got to Nadia's room, Hayes was gone. Bri knew she would have headed back to the lab immediately, wanting to keep the chain of custody with the evidence intact. She also remembered Hayes had wanted to go over the stomach contents analysis from Max's body, and Bri made a mental note to stop there on the way back from the hospital.

The girl's head was swathed in bandages, her eyes still swollen. She had been cleaned and dressed in a hospital gown, Bri assumed after Hayes had conducted her examination. Nadia sat up in bed, hands folded in her lap, an IV-line pumping antibiotics and fluid into her.

Petra rushed to the girl's side, embracing her with the utmost care. Nadia murmured reassurances to Petra. Finally, Trent pulled a chair over for Petra to sit and looked to Bri.

Inhaling, Bri tried her best smile. "Hello again, Nadia. I'm really sorry for what has happened, but we were wondering if you were up to answering a couple questions?"

Nadia nodded, a ferocity crossing her face. "Yes, Inspector. I learned a long time ago if I keep quiet, I am only allowing the control to revert back to my attackers. They are cowards."

"If at any time, this gets too much, please tell us and we'll stop."

Nadia nodded, slipping her hand into Petra's.

"Do you remember what happened yesterday?"

"I left the tutoring center and I was approached by an Asian man…he was young, but I'm not sure how old he really was. He was nervous and asked me if I had a cigarette. I don't smoke, so I said so and I tried to pass him."

"Then what happened?" Bri had pulled out her trusty notepad to jot down the details.

"He elbowed me in the stomach and dragged me off the street."

Bri arched a brow, glancing to Trent. They both had the same question on their minds—how had no one seen this?

"He started to beat me, but a man from the street intervened…the guy hitting me ran off. I thought the man would help me…but he knelt down instead and said I deserved it, and that it was just a warning."

Bri's lips compacted into a fine line. So, it was a planned attack…and it was sending a message. But how had they found out about Nadia's participation in the investigation? Someone must have leaked information or had seen them meeting. But who could it have been? Bri trusted Trent and Hayes implicitly, and neither would risk a case by collaborating with any criminal.

"Thank you for your help, Nadia. We'll make sure an officer stays with you. The hospital has already been apprised of the situation, and they will make sure you are safe." Bri closed the notepad and gave Trent a meaningful look. As if mentally connected, he nodded. They had a lot to discuss.

"I'll stay with Nadia, Inspectors. I want to make sure she has everything she needs." Petra was firm in her affirmation, and Bri thought how lucky the girls were to have her.

"All right, Ms. Vasquez. We'll be in touch. Call if you need anything." Bri followed Trent out into the corridor.

"What are you thinking?" He dropped his voice, conscious of the medical staff milling around.

Bri scanned them as they passed, trying to commit faces to memory. "I think we have a rat."

"Yeah, but who? No one, aside from you, me, Meyers, and Kastner knows what's going on." Trent hooked his thumbs into the pockets of his dark jeans.

"I don't know yet." Bri rubbed the back of her neck before loosening her ponytail slightly; the tension in her hair was starting to match that of the tension in her head. "In any case, we need to see Hayes, so let's go do that now. I need to think."

They fell into step, Trent whistling under his breath as they headed back to the parking lot. Bri knew he could feel it too. They were that in sync—a nearly perfect partnership. It would come to one—or both of them—in time. The niggling uncertainty that they were being watched—that someone was hiding something from them.

*** * ***

Hayes was at her desk when the inspectors ambled in. "How's the girl doing?"

Bri landed in one of the chairs in front of the desk, while Trent did his usual lean against Hayes' filing cabinet. "She appears wholly optimistic about the situation. It seems she was targeted to send a warning to us."

"Pretty bold, I'd say." Standing, Hayes went to the cabinet, glaring at Trent, who held up his hands meekly and stepped away. She opened one drawer, replaced a file, and withdrew another. While most of the information on cases was kept on computer, Hayes still preferred to keep paper copies of research papers which might help her decipher the evidence.

"So, the analysis…?"

"Yes, I'm getting there." She smiled and sat down. "We recovered some samples from Max's stomach…"

Bri appreciated how Hayes humanized the victims of crime, especially when the case involved a child. "Go on."

"They have an interesting chemical composition." She placed a paper on the desk and Trent and Bri looked it over, knowing that the spikes on the graph indicated levels of…something.

"Gonna have to dumb it down for those of us who don't speak chemistry," Trent quipped.

Hayes rolled her eyes. "I was going to, Billy. I don't expect *you* to have this level of understanding." The good-natured barb hit home, and Trent clutched his chest in mock injury.

The break of laughter felt good and alleviated some of

the tension surrounding all three.

"Admittedly, I didn't know what I was looking at, at first. Then I overheard one of the CSIs talking about how alcohol has different compositions. Apparently, he went to a wine tasting course in Napa over the weekend. I knew it was a solution of ethanol and water in some form, so I took a gamble. Started fishing around in my own chemistry journals, and when that gave little insight, I took to the internet." Hayes made a face. She hated the consolidation of information accessible to the masses and how anyone could post anything, and someone would believe it. Still, she recognized the value of the internet as a source.

"And what did you find?"

"An article dating back to 2010 about an experiment done by a group of German chemists about the chemical composition of various vodkas." Hayes angled her chair back, a pleased smile forming on her lips.

"Whoa, wait, vodka's vodka, right?" Trent lifted his eyebrows. "Fermented potatoes?"

"It can also be made from grains, actually. You're so cultured, Billy." The comment sent Hayes and Bri into further fits of giggles.

"It was only the girls who drank the stuff in college. Coors man all the way." Trent crossed his arms with a cocky smile reminiscent of a frat boy.

Bri threw a pencil at him. "Come on, Cat, break it down for us."

"Well, while vodkas all contain the same key ingredients, it's the level of each ingredient which distinguishes one brand from another." Hayes very much resembled the proverbial cat who got the cream. "And…luckily, we have managed to get some different brands to test."

Both inspectors angled their bodies forward in anticipation. "Well?" Bri couldn't handle the building suspense, and when Hayes revealed the name, she nearly fell out of her chair.

"Are you sure?"

"Yes, positive. It's hard to tell exactly, but I would hypothesize that Max was intoxicated at the time of his death." Hayes frowned, eyeing up Bri, who knew her face had turned a shade of green, her stomach churning. "You know where Max's body was kept?"

"Yeah, I do."

32
LINA

Leon is here. In this house. For the first time, I let the voice take over after Korschev releases me from under his weight. I walk back to my room in a daze.

We can get our revenge. He put us here.

I shake my head, wanting to cry. I fell for this man's manipulations. I dragged Max to a foreign country based on a girlish whim.

I bet he's the one taking us to a new place.

"Stop!"

A few of the girls look up at me as I enter the room, having stopped in the doorway to make my outburst. One hushes me. Another rolls over on her cot.

"Aren't you glad to see me, Lina?" Leon's chest is pressed against my back, hands rubbing down my arms.

He's behind you! Let me play, Little Lina.

I cast my eyes downward, submissive. I hate myself. I hate the pain and stickiness between my thighs. Shame sweeps over me.

"You still look so beautiful."

A spark flickers in my chest, and my head shoots up,

the anger on the tip of my tongue. Then I remember the girl who got pregnant. I remember the photographs, and the spark extinguishes.

"Tomorrow, you are going to come with me. I have a special client for you." Leon runs a finger down my cheek. I want to scrub the feeling away that lingers after his touch has lifted.

Is anything worth it anymore? Why not hurt someone before he hurts you?

"See you then."

Before I can react, he is gone.

33

Kastner emerged from Captain Meyers' office as Bri and Trent entered the building. They met at the elevator.

"Hey, Kastner, we have some new information…" Bri barely got the words out before he held up a hand.

"Sorry, I have to go meet with my superiors." He brushed past them into the open elevator, jabbing his finger onto the 'close door' button with ferocity, his face a mask as the doors slid shut.

"What the heck was that?" Trent cocked his head.

"No idea. Let's go report to Meyers." Bri wound her way through the desks to the office door of their Captain. After a quick knock and a gruff admission of entry, the pair stood before Meyers' desk, perplexed at the dark look crossing the stern features of his face.

"So, you want to explain?"

Trent looked at Bri, befuddled. "Sir?"

"About how a witness in our case was tracked down and attacked? Didn't you put safety measures in place?"

Bri undoubtably knew Trent would feel her temper bubbling, and sure enough, he cut in. "It wasn't like that, Cap. Ms. Vasquez said she didn't want any other security. She didn't want to draw attention to the women in her shelter."

"You should have put surveillance in place!"

"We have officers at the hospital now. The witness is secure, sir. There's not much more we can do at this point. Besides," he tried his best conciliatory grin. Bri knew it well. It was one he put on when he wanted to use his male comradery to put Meyers in a better mood. "We have news back from Dr. Hayes about evidence found on the first body."

"Go on." Meyers tapped a pen on a stack of folders in front of him, his irritation tangible.

"Hayes thinks it's vodka, sir."

Even the usually stoic captain couldn't stop the incredulity from crossing his face. "Vodka? What sort of bullshit is this?"

Bri, exasperated, chimed in. "It's true, sir. And I think it may have ties to the Russian bistro Kastner and I visited the other night, the Little Russian Tea Room."

"What makes you think that? Vodka is pretty commonplace, Inspector Ryu. That's a rather large leap."

"Not really." Bri smirked inwardly. "We know Sokolov has ties to the Russian Mafia. We know Korschev—another suspected Mafia member—was speaking to him the night Kastner and I were there, referencing the moving of a girl. We also know Sokolov prides himself on his vodka collection, and Hayes informed us vodka varies in chemical composition based on the specific brand. And he keeps it in a deep freeze. That's the best way to taste vodka, apparently."

"We'd need a warrant to search the premises. I think we can get one based on the tapes and the statement you put together from the undercover operation, as well as the fact the body was frozen prior to being disposed of. Where is Kastner?"

Bri hated thinking of Max being disposed of, like a piece of garbage. "He said he had to go deal with his superiors."

Meyers grumbled. "Damned Feds. I'll get on the horn to the DA and get back to you. In the meantime, I'll need the brand name of the vodka. And we have to make sure that Sokolov stocks it at his bistro. Can you attest to that?"

Bri handed over the evidence report. "It's Stolichnaya Elit. I tasted it while I was there."

Meyers picked up the phone. "Right. I'll get a warrant for you to seize a bottle from his store for comparison to Hayes' sample. Although I don't know how well it will hold up in court. Still, keep your eyes open while you're there. Maybe you'll catch something that will give us further probable cause."

With that, they were summarily dismissed. Bri griped as she crossed to her desk. "This is like chasing ghosts."

"What do you mean? We're getting a warrant."

"Yeah, but I can't shake this feeling."

Trent sat in his desk chair, pulling out a pack of Reese's Peanut Butter Cups from his desk drawer. "You always have a feeling. What I want to know is what's going on between you and Ms. Vasquez."

Flinging a paperclip at him, Bri felt the color rising in her cheeks. "She's involved in an active investigation, so nothing."

"Liar, liar pants on fire."

The second paperclip made a connection with his head. "Shut up."

"Hey, those things are like gold dust around here. Cutbacks, ya know!" He held his hand up defensively, his mouth full of chocolate.

"Then stop annoying me!"

Trent grew placid. "Seriously, what is up with her? Is she…ya know?" He twirled a hand in the air.

"Gay? Yeah, I think so…" Bri made a point of refocusing her attention on the growing list of emails in her inbox.

"So…" He waggled his eyebrows.

"You perv." She took aim with another paperclip.

Trent held up his hands in defeat. "All right, all right. I give." He rocked back in his chair, propping his feet on his desk. "Still…it's been a while…"

"Ugh, you and Cat. I swear…I'm fine on my own. Really. When do I have time for all that romance people expect? I mean, look at you and Christine. It doesn't work. Us and them."

"But she's not really a 'them,' Bri. She's used to this sector." Another whole peanut butter cup disappeared between his lips.

Meticulously deleting department bulletins, charity requests, and happy birthday messages, Bri took a few moments to contemplate his words. He had an uncanny way of delivering the truth, even through a mouthful of masticated peanut butter and chocolate. She smiled, remembering him telling her it was his favorite candy when they first became partners. A bond developed from them, as she snuck them into his desk drawer on occasion, enjoying the surprise on his face when he discovered them. Eventually, he cottoned on to her secretive practice, but he never stopped it. It was their tradition.

"Maybe after this case is done…"

"'Atta girl!" Trent folded the cardboard support from the orange candy wrapper into triangles—his ritual—before pinging it into the trash.

"And you?" Bri lifted her eyes from the screen.

Trent shrugged. "Plenty of fish in the sea. There's a new tech…"

She groaned. "Oh, no, Billy, not a coworker…"

"I said tech…CSI…whatever. We don't work in the same office." He grinned. "She's cute…blonde, petite…"

"A little cheerleader for your…" She flicked her eyes

downward, and this time, it was Trent who fired a paperclip.

"Low blow, Bri."

"Literally." She began to laugh as her cell phone rang. "Ryu." Her smile was replaced with a deep-set frown. "I see. We'll be there soon. Hold him until we do."

Trent swiped the back of his hand over his mouth, removing all traces of his sugar boost. "What's up?"

"Someone tried to break into the ward."

* * *

Petra was frantic—a state Bri had never seen her in before—by the time the two inspectors arrived at the ward. The officer on duty had a man wearing dark blue scrubs cuffed in a plastic hospital chair, while his partner milled around, hands in his utility belt, looking decidedly mean.

"He…had an ID badge…I was about to go to the bathroom, but this feeling I had made me stay. He tried to get me to leave, saying he needed to do something to…" Petra trembled violently.

Trent touched Bri's shoulder. "Maybe take her into the family room? I'll deal with the perp." He sauntered over to the uniforms, both grinning at his approach.

"Damned frat boy mentality," Bri muttered to herself, as she turned back to Petra, guiding her to a small room.

As the door closed, Petra collapsed into Bri's arms, sobbing. All she could do was console the woman, who was scared beyond her wits. It was a good ten minutes before Petra could form a coherent sentence.

"I'm sorry. What you must think of me…" Petra wiped her sleeve over her eyes.

Bri's heart ached for her. She wondered if Petra had fully dealt with all the trauma of her own experiences before giving herself over to the girls in her care. It wasn't uncommon. She had heard of support workers using their jobs to cope with their own demons. All it took was one trigger for them to come face to face with them in vibrant color, instead of the vague shades of gray. It was detachment for self-preservation.

"I don't think anything bad of you, Petra. You're human. You've been through as much trauma as any of those girls. You did the right thing, though. You're a good person." Bri rubbed her back, brushing back a strand of ebony hair which had stuck to the woman's damp cheek. It was a supremely intimate gesture, but Bri knew the woman next to her needed some human compassion.

"I…knew…when I saw him that he was bad. He had a glint in his eye I recognized from the men before. His scrubs also didn't fit him. They were wrinkled, not pressed like the other nurses and doctors. Thank goodness Nadia was asleep."

Bri was suitably impressed. "You have a good eye, Petra." She took the woman's hand, and Petra was apparently content to let it linger in Bri's.

She hiccupped and smiled. "Yes…you notice things when you're not allowed to speak."

The line began to blur as Bri was distinctly aware of the connection from their touching hands. "What did you do to cope?"

"You…what's the word…disassociate. Yes, that's what the counselors said when I was rescued." Petra's fingers fluttered against Bri's.

Bri now understood why Trent had made the decision for her to deal with Petra. *Damn it, Trent. You're not Cupid.* She sighed, seeing that she had missed human connection more than she had let on. Hayes and Trent were great, but there was a level of intimacy which couldn't be provided by them—that heart-skipping moment which sent her pulse skittering into her throat. She quelled it, detangling her fingers from Petra's, hesitating as she saw the woman's face fall.

"Oh…no, I…"

"You have to be professional; I understand." The smile didn't hide the hurt in her captivating eyes.

Bri impulsively snatched Petra's hand again. "After…all this…can we, maybe, go for drinks together?" Hayes would be doing backflips that Bri was putting herself out there again, but she imagined the tutting when she found out who it was with. Trent would just give her an infuriating *I-told-you-so* smile.

Petra's eyes lightened, the hurt vanishing like the fog around the Bridge on a sunny day. "Yes, I would like that. Or maybe a walk in the park?"

The change in demeanor had her smiling genuinely. "Even better." Bri reviled the thought of shouting over the patrons in a bar. "Now, I have to take your statement. Then we'll talk to the officers and take the suspect into custody."

Petra nodded, as Bri took out her notebook. "I understand."

"Good. Let's start at the beginning…"

* * *

By the time Bri emerged from the room, the two officers and Trent were shooting the breeze about one of the recent basketball games, Trent mimicking a jump shot as the officers laughed. The man in the chair had his head down, his stringy black hair obscuring his face. They had cuffed his hands to the chair, preventing all but the most humorous of escape attempts.

Finally, the three men noticed her presence, and Petra emerging just behind her. Her eyes had hardened, and the idiom 'If looks could kill' most certainly applied. Bri was sure if she had less self-control, Petra would have throttled the man then and there.

Trent detached himself from his fawning fan club and walked over to them. "So…can we book him?"

"Yeah."

He motioned to the two officers. "Book him and leave him in a holding cell at Central. Keep him on watch too. No fuck-ups, gentlemen."

One officer unlocked the cuffs holding the man to the chair, and the other hoisted him up by the arm. "Catch ya later, Trent." They none-too-gently escorted the thin Asian man from the hospital.

"I could kill him." Petra's fists clenched.

"What?" Trent peered between Petra and Bri, confused.

Bri sighed. "Before Petra screamed and pressed the alert button, he spoke to her."

"Yeah?"

"He said, 'You'll never find her.'"

34

Sokolov sat in his corner booth, chewing on a manicured thumbnail. Awaiting news was the most frustrating part of his role in this convoluted circle of corruption. He wanted to break free, but how could he? The money coming in from the Mafia was good, and they could easily ruin him. If he told the FBI he was out, he would end up in prison. It was a mess—his mess. But what choice did he have? Had he rejected Korschev's initial offer, the entire balloon would have gone up. He could testify. No. That would be suicide.

His niece approached, handing him a drink. She looked decidedly bored until a handsome young man appeared at the door. Immediately, Sokolov was on alert. He had Slavic features and warning bells began to blare in the depths of his mind. First the unsolicited visit from Agent Kastner, then the undercover operation—where had he found the beautiful Asian woman who had accompanied him?—and then Korschev's request to house one of his girls, albeit temporarily. It was all getting too much for his blood pressure. He watched the interaction of the man and his niece through veiled lids, trying not to look like he was paying too much attention.

162

When the man touched Galena's hand, he jumped up, nearly upsetting his glass.

"Galena! Go to the back."

Her petulant expression reminded him of his wife when she didn't get her way.

"Now!"

She rolled her eyes, snapped her gum, and moved off, pulling out her cell phone, thumbs flying over the screen.

"There was no need for that, Mr. Sokolov." The young man's smile unnerved him. "Mr. Korschev sends his deepest regards, to you, your wife, and your niece. She's lovely, is she not?"

Sokolov knew it could reach this point one day. It was just a matter of time. His easy ride was about to come to a jarring halt. "She is. So much potential."

"Mr. Korschev has spoken of her a few times since the tasting party. He extends his gratitude and asks if preparations are in place for your agreed contract?"

Sokolov nodded, almost too quickly. "Yes, I have a room prepared upstairs…locks on the outside… Did Mr. Korschev state how long I would be holding her?" He wrung his hands, feeling the sweat pooling at the base of his spine, dampening his otherwise crisp shirt.

"No, nor should it be any concern of yours." The man smiled, his fang-like canines glinting. He was a *volk*, a wolf. Sokolov knew immediately he was one who would be used by Korschev to 'recruit' his women.

"Yes, of course…I merely wonder in case my employees are to ask…"

"She's a relative. No more, no less." The man stood. "Remember, Mr. Sokolov, we are watching."

Sokolov's bravado returned. He wasn't going to be pushed around in his own premises. He deserved to know who was threatening his livelihood. "And what do I call you?"

The muscles in the man's jaw rippled, before his smile

returned, predatory as ever. "Leon. My name is Leon."

35
LINA

The clock on Korschev's wall ticks louder, drowning out my heartbeat. We are waiting for Leon to return. He's gone to the place they are taking me. How will Max find me now? Will they tell him where I've been taken?

Don't be stupid, girl. Take his pen and stab him. Run.

I wish the voice would quiet. He—yes, I have figured out that it's male—has become louder in the past day, since Korschev raped me on his desk. I am not so silly to think this is repayment of debt, and therefore, I have given unspoken consent to have my body violated over and over.

I feel uncomfortable in the jeans and hoodie. I'm not used to being so covered. The shoes on my feet are new. I smile inwardly.

New shoes…what a treat. Makes up for all the fucking, doesn't it?

"Oh, shut up," I think I have spoken under my breath, but I realize with abject horror that I've spoken aloud. Korschev is looking at me.

"I…I am sorry, sir. The clock…is…loud." My words

come haltingly. I feel stupid. I am stupid. Stupid, stupid, stupid.

He grunts, brushing off my comments, thankfully, as the babbling nonsense of a girl who has been starved and beaten and abused.

The door to the office opens, and we both jump.

"Damn it, Leon. Knock next time!" Korschev growls. "Well?"

"All is ready. I'm going to move her tonight." They speak as if I am not there. I am a mannequin, a husk, a silent observer.

Just attack! Who would want you now, little Lina?

Shut up. I remember not to voice my retort aloud this time.

"And Sokolov?"

"Complacent. You're right. His niece is lovely. Unfortunate that she should be tied to a family who would no doubt miss her presence."

"I wasn't thinking of her for the job, idiot."

Leon frowns. "I don't understand."

"We need a hold on Sokolov. I do not trust him at all. You like her, don't you?"

Why do they talk like I'm not here? Oh, yes, I'm not here. I'm an object. Like the desk. Or the filing cabinet.

"I guess she's all right. Young."

"Then, she's your new responsibility. Woo her. Marry her. It's for the family. You understand?"

Leon looks upset, irritated even, but he will comply. They all do.

"Good." He gestures to me. "Take her now."

Leon's hand circles my arm, tightening, hoisting me from the chair. "One wrong move, bitch, and I filet you and feed you to the fishes."

I quake. I have to survive. I have to find out what happened to Max. I nod.

Coward.

36

The interrogation room at Central was cramped and windowless. A camera light blinked in the corner and the recorder was embedded in the wall, modern technology at its finest. Bri stretched out her legs, chewing on the end of a pen, studying the file in front of her. It contained the booking information for the man, who had been identified via his fingerprints as Colin Chang, along with a slew of aliases. He had been convicted of petty theft prior to this in Chinatown, but had remained off the radar since then, despite being suspected in several other cases, including possible associations with the Triad organization. He had been Mirandized and declined the right to counsel.

"So, Mr. Chang, do you want to tell us what you were doing at St. Francis earlier today?" They had left him to sweat in the holding cell for a few hours, hoping the pressure would provoke more forthcoming answers to their questions, as well as allowing them to make a positive ID via his prints.

"No comment."

She heard Trent groan next to her. This was going to be a long one, and she didn't have time to pander to someone who thought he was hot shit. Bri knew when to cut her losses, but she had one more trick up her sleeve.

"Very well." She began to pack up her folder and stood. "We have enough to charge him on trespassing as well as fraud. Also, suspected aggravated assault."

Chang widened his eyes, his pock-marked skin glinting with sweat. "What...I..."

Bri faced him again, eyes hard. "Was there something else, Mr. Chang?"

The tactic made those with too much to lose often loosen up.

"I..."

"You have a wife and son, yes?"

Chang rubbed his hands on the wrinkled pants of the borrowed scrubs. Even in the winter, sweat pooled and left dark marks on his underarms. "Yes..."

"They need your financial support, don't they? It's not easy to live in the Bay Area without adequate income."

"No..."

Bri sat down again. "So, are you going to cooperate with us? We would very much hate to see your son and wife homeless and destitute."

It was a low blow, but Bri had little sympathy for men who preyed on women. She had no doubt in her mind this was also the man who had attacked Nadia. As soon as they were finished here, they would show her a picture of the man and hope she would be brave enough to positively identify him in a line-up—and even braver still to testify against him in court.

"If I tell you what I know, you'll give me...uh...what is it called...?"

"Immunity? Possibly. It would certainly make your case more sympathetic in the eyes of the DA."

"Okay, okay...I was hired by a man to get the girl."

"Why her?"

"She talked to you."

Bri sat back down, hoping her face remained neutral. Trent took over. "Talked to us? You're going to have to clarify that, Mr. Chang."

"They saw you, at the gardens, talking."

"And who is they?" Trent's pen was poised.

"I want protective custody." Chang had grown a set of balls pretty quickly. He crossed his arms. Bri knew he wouldn't budge.

"We'll see what we can arrange. Now, who are they?"

Chang opened his mouth, but a swift knock, followed by Meyers' entry, had Bri grumbling under her breath. He was followed by a man in a tacky pinstripe suit, white collar dingy in the crappy lighting.

"Inspectors, Mr. Chang has retained his right to counsel."

Bri's mouth nearly dropped open. "What?" She looked to Trent who shrugged. "We have his signed refusal to retain counsel right here!" She held up the form with Chang's chicken scratch at the bottom.

"My client has nothing further to say." The man's slicked back hair was about as greasy as his entire demeanor.

"We are still going to be pressing charges." Trent stood and cuffed Chang. "You can see your client again when he goes before a judge in the morning."

The sleazebag lawyer started to protest, but Meyers cut him off, appearing no less pleased about this than Bri did. "My inspector is correct. We have protocol to follow as well, Mr. Rossi. You can meet your client in the morning," he reiterated, hammering the point home.

Trent escorted Chang out, followed by Rossi. Bri turned to Meyers. "What the heck is going on, sir?"

"Don't know, Ryu, but I want to double the watch around your witness in the hospital. This man appeared at the front desk, demanding to see his client. I, too, was under the impression that he had waived his right to counsel. Since he didn't object now, we'll just have to hold him and see what the judge says in the morning." Meyers nodded sympathetically and left the interrogation room. It was only once the door had shut that Bri cursed loudly.

"FUCK!"

* * *

After the interview with Chang, there wasn't much left to do. Trent and Bri were worn out, having worked the case for nearly a week solid without much rest. Trent offered to show the photograph to Nadia at St. Francis on his way home, practically ordering Bri back to her lonely apartment.

After a hot shower, she lounged on the couch, the TV droning on as background noise, an untouched glass of red wine on the table in front of her. Loneliness hit her like a fastball pitch at AT&T Park. She picked up and put down the phone a dozen times, wanting to call her grandfather, but knowing he would never pick up one of her calls again. She reclined on the couch, phone resting on her chest, and closed her eyes. The tears were unexpected, starting with a tingling in her nose as they fell over her cheeks, almost burning as they moistened her dry, tired eyes.

The knock on the door had her sitting bolt upright and contemplating going for her duty weapon, locked in the safe in her bedroom. She opted instead for the Maglite she kept by the door. If anything, it would club any potential attacker to death, and after Chang's revelation they were being watched, she was taking no chances.

Bri looked through the peephole, surprised to see Petra standing on the opposite side of her door. *How did she get my address?* She cautiously opened it, hand still on the Maglite. "Uh, hi?"

Petra glanced left, and then right. "Sorry…I didn't mean to come to your home… Inspector Trent said it would be fine…"

Damn it, Billy! This is a murder investigation! Not 'let's play matchmaker with my partner.'

Bri sighed, pushing open the door entirely. "Come on in." She tried her best for a smile but knew her eyes would be red from the unexpected bout of tears.

"I'm sorry," Petra apologized again. "Is this a bad time?"

Bri shut the door, checking the deadbolt and then showing her into the spartan living room. "No, no, it's just…irregular, that's all. I shouldn't have you here. I could get into a lot of trouble, protocol wise. In fact, I should tell you to go right now."

"I…know. Truly, I do. I wanted to talk to you…without all the protocol. Maybe I should have waited." She was taking in the room, then Bri, who was conscious of her underdressed appearance, hair hanging damp to her shoulders. She never let it grow much longer than that as it drove her crazy.

Finally, Bri capitulated. "Come on, have a seat. Wine?"

Petra shook her head. "No, I don't drink, actually. I think it's a side effect from having been forced to drink so much when—" The words, although left unspoken, were clear to both parties.

"Right." Bri picked up the glass and summarily tipped it into the sink before returning to sit on the couch, one cushion between her and Petra. "So…"

Nervous laughter blurted out from both.

"This is silly." Petra smiled, her hands in her lap. Her gray slacks were wrinkled, as was her lilac blouse, probably from spending so much time at the hospital and not enough at home.

"It is. Umm, how's Nadia doing?"

"Oh, very good. She was fine with the photograph Trent showed her, and she wants to pick him out of a line up."

"Yeah, I do think she's going to have to go into protective custody after this, though. I mean, not that I don't trust your shelter…"

Petra shifted, angling her body toward Bri. "I understand."

The strained silence between them blanketed the room. There was tension between them, Bri knew that. She didn't think it was bad tension either, but it was like a rubber band pulled too tightly, ready to snap with the tiniest touch.

Petra inched onto the cushion next to Bri. "I put too much pressure on you. I'm sorry."

"Please, stop apologizing." Bri grasped the other woman's hand. "I know that stress provokes different reactions in people. I—"

Her final sentence was cut off by Petra cupping Bri's cheek and kissing her. As their lips met, a thought entered the back of Bri's mind. *No going back now.*

37

Bri groggily came to life at the ringing of her cell phone. This was becoming too much of a trend now. Only this time, she wasn't alone in bed, as she fumbled for the irritating device. She smiled, seeing Petra's sleeping face on the pillow next to her, hair a mass of sexy waves. The smile broke into a grin as she answered the call, tiptoeing from the room.

"Ryu."

"Heeeeeey, how's the love connection?"

Groaning, Bri shut the bedroom door and padded into the bathroom, suddenly aware of her nakedness. Not like Trent could see her through the phone. "Why did you give her my address? And I hope no one can hear you! It could blow our case, you irresponsible…"

"I'm in my car. Answer the question!"

Bri slipped into an oversized T-shirt she'd left discarded on the bathroom floor. "Fine, because I know you won't stop hounding me, and neither will Cat once she gets wind of your shenanigans."

"Well, if anything, you needed to get laid."

Sitting on the toilet lid, Bri rested her elbows on her knees. "Not everything is solved by getting laid!" *Typical man.* Although she'd never admit it to him, she did feel better. Her head had cleared, and her muscles felt less tense. The endorphins released during sex were no lie. "Anyway, what do you want?"

"Warrant came through. Thought you'd want to know we're planning to do a little rattlin' cages this afternoon."

The bathroom door creaked open and Petra stood there, wrapped in the top sheet from Bri's bed. They shared a secretive smile, before Petra made the universal motion for coffee. Bri nodded and returned her attention back to Trent. "Yeah, sounds good."

"Cool. See ya then."

She growled as he made kissing noises and hung up. Shaking her head, she breathed in, the scent of coffee filling her nostrils. She found Petra in the kitchen, still wrapped in the sheet, having knotted it around her breasts in a toga-like fashion. There was no awkwardness between them. Bri simply slipped her arms around the other woman's waist from behind and kissed her neck, breathing in the scent she had earmarked as uniquely Petra's.

"This is crazy, you know."

Petra let out a husky laugh. "You know what's even crazier? You have nothing in your fridge. How is that possible?"

Bri rested her chin on Petra's shoulder. "I betcha you don't either."

"Fair enough. Shower then breakfast? My treat."

It was nice being like this. Even with her other partners, Bri had never felt as at ease as she was in this moment. Denial of her feelings were simply self-preservation methods she'd developed to keep the emotional ache from sinking its claws into her. Allowing herself to be truly vulnerable with a person was a rarity, and Bri sensed that Petra was exactly the same. In knowing Petra's past, she may have not wanted to trigger anything in the woman, but to her surprise, Petra had been the more dominant of the pair. Bri kissed her neck again and wondered what surprises she would have in store as the relationship progressed—*if* it progressed.

"Do you need to hurry off? I should have asked."

Bri released her and reached for the coffee mug. "Sorry, lost in a world of my own. Yeah, I will this afternoon. We have a warrant to search a…" She clammed up.

Petra sipped her coffee. "I understand. Please, don't feel like I have to know everything."

Silence lapsed before Bri took in the woman before her, tousle-haired, wrapped in a sheet, a strange vulnerable beauty emanating from her person. Right and wrong bounced around her mind, knowing she'd crossed the line of professionalism, giving in to both their needs. It was as if the unspoken thoughts had been given voice, as Petra took Bri's hand in her own.

"I knew what I was doing when I came here last night. Until everything is wrapped up with this case…with Nadia…I know what we have to do. But I just had to see…I had to know if it was real."

Bri felt the corners of her mouth tug up. "It was real, I promise. I want to see where things go with us…but you're right. Until the paperwork is signed, and Nadia goes to court to testify against this guy, we need to keep things strictly by the book."

Petra adopted a coy expression, so unlike her usual personality. She tugged Bri closer. "One more for the road?"

There was little resistance as she led Bri back to bed.

38
LINA

The evening air vibrates around me as I walk alongside Leon. I am like a child, seeing the world for the first time. After a few twisting blocks, he lets me lift my eyes to the great city. San Francisco, I know it now. How could I have been here for so long and not noticed? I want to grab the first person I see and beg for help, but I think of Max. What would they do to him if I were to be so careless?

Leon's face is hard, and I think of the girl they were talking about. She would be drawn in, not as a victim...but a wife. A wife who would probably be showered with all the luxury in the world, while I bleed and suffer at the hands of her husband, or other men like him.

Run.

I will the voice to silence.

Remember what he did to you? He was the first. Your first.

Stop. Please. Enough. Let me get to where I'm going. Then I can think.

Not if he's taking you to your death.

My feet refuse to move. Leon looks at me, irritation spreading on his handsome features. Instead of speaking, he steps forward. To the passersby, it looks like he's merely resting a hand on my arm. His fingers dig into the soft underside. "Come on," he whispers, his voice dark and menacing. I have no choice but to comply.

As we round a corner, he yanks me back, away from the bustle of a gathering crowd. A strangled cry holds in my throat, as he clamps a hand over my mouth.

"Shut up!"

He pulls out his cell phone, punching in a number.

"We have a problem."

39

Korschev swore as he hung up the phone. The police had surrounded Sokolov's establishment and had drawn a crowd to boot! His beefy fist hit the desk, causing pens to judder and papers to float to the floor. "*Blyad!* Fuck!"

He rose and began to pace, agitated, feeling his blood pressure rising. His face heated considerably. This was a mess. Ever since that boy had gone to the police in a vain attempt to get help for him and his sister, everything had been going wrong. Still, as long as they kept it from Lina that her brother was dead, they could get her to do whatever they wanted. Luckily, she had struck the interest of a man with the means to purchase her from him.

Korschev smiled at the thought of two million American dollars hitting his offshore bank account. It would be enough to fund several trips back to Ukraine, for the recruitment of more girls, more fake passports, more facilities. With measured breaths, his blood pressure returned to normal. There was always another plan, another way to make things work. He had been evading law enforcement for ten years now. There was no way he was going to let some SFPD inspector bring him down.

Sitting and spinning his chair, he steepled his fingers.

"Inspector Briana Ryu." His informant had been thorough. Of course, as usual, mild pressure had to be applied, as in all cases. He knew Sokolov would require some convincing as well in regard to his niece. Gaining footholds in the community and expanding his business enterprises were always thoughts on his mind—every opportunity must be explored, every chance to gain new allies helped keep the money flowing in.

Then there were the constant thorns in his side. Petra Vasquez was one. He chuckled to himself, thinking how unaware the police were of his reach—his intel on the city he kept under his thumb. He picked up the phone and dialed Leon's cell phone.

"Where are you?" There was no time for pleasantries.

"Same spot, boss."

"Good. Take her back to your apartment and watch her. She won't do anything. If she tries it, remind her we know where her brother is—and if she wants to see him alive again, she'll do what we say."

"But…boss…"

"Just do it, Leon. I'll deal with Sokolov."

* * *

Bri waited behind one of the patrol cars as the SWAT team cleared the building. Sokolov—the owner—blustered and demanded to know the reason for this unreasonable search. Why did people always think that things were like they were on TV? Warrants weren't issued on a whim. They had had valid evidence to obtain theirs, and no judge would have put his robes on the line for anything less. She glanced around at the gathered uniforms and forensic technicians, headed by Hayes, and frowned.

"Where's Kastner? I'd've thought this would have been his cup of tea."

Trent shrugged, playing a game on his cell phone.

"No clue. I left him, like, five messages, including a text. He didn't answer."

"Strange. When we get back to the station, remind me to call his supervisor. I've got a feeling…"

"Wooo hooo! That tonight's gonna be a good night…" Trent chuckled as he sang off-key.

Bri elbowed him. "Seriously, though, I think something is up."

"You always have a feeling. I would've thought after last night, some of that tension would've loosened up." Trent grinned and waggled his eyebrows.

Bri gritted her teeth. "Shut up, you idiot."

Meyers, who had insisted on leading the operation, approached Bri and Trent and they straightened. "All clear. I'm sending in Hayes and her team first. Then you can go."

Bri slumped back on the patrol car as Meyers walked away. "Great. Why did we agree to this song and dance again?"

"Because of Sokolov's suspected connections to the Mafia. We didn't want to fall into any traps," Trent stated matter-of-factly. "Duh. Usual bureaucratic bullshit."

"CYA, you mean. Cover your ass."

"Exactly. A dead officer or *inspector* wouldn't look good for Meyers, would it?" Trent shoved his phone into his pocket.

"Yeah, yeah." She looked up as a uniform ran over. "What is it?"

"Cap just got a call. A body's been found. Male."

Bri observed the operation with a disgruntled groan. "Can't someone else handle it?"

"Cap said you'd want to. Personally." The uniform was fresh-faced, the idealistic optimism of a new recruit, ready to change the city single-handedly. He bounced eagerly on the balls of his feet. Bri wondered how quickly those dreams would be crushed—like Lina and Max's dreams had been.

Trent's low rumbling tone broke her reverie. "Why did he say that?"

The uniform shrugged. "Dunno, sir. He just said…"

Bri thought about protesting but realized it would probably not accomplish anything. "Fine, we'll go. Where's the locus?"

"Body is at Stockton Street."

"Chinatown?" Trent cast Bri a look out of the corner of his eye.

"Yeah, I think so. He wants you to go ASAP." The uniform headed off back in the direction of the action.

Trent tugged Bri's arm in the direction of their car. "Come on. I'm gonna give you three guesses who they found, and the first two don't count."

Bri's fingertips start to tingle as a cold sweat broke out on her body. "Shit, shit, shit! We should've guessed when that slimy lawyer came into the station."

"We don't know for sure, but I'd bet my badge on it." Trent seated himself on the driver's side—and for once, Bri didn't protest.

*** * ***

The scene was straightforward. No one had taken time to process the body like they had with Max. It was a clear message—so clear, in fact, that it was pinned to the victim's chest in loopy handwriting: *If you value her life, stay away, Inspector Ryu.*

Bri shuddered, pressing a hand to her stomach, the light-headed feeling returning with a vengeance.

Trent noted the marked change in his partner and hurried to deal with the techs and uniforms on site. Then he returned to her side. Bri hadn't moved—she couldn't move.

"He knows we're after him. Lina is in danger." She lifted her eyes, looking up at Trent. "How does he know?"

"I'm sure he's a man with fingers in many pies, Bri," Trent kept his voice low, reassuring. "No doubt he knew since the first time you met Max at the station."

"It's Korschev. I know it. There's no other explanation."

"But how could he know it was us investigating? The only time he met you was at that undercover operation with…"

"Kastner." Bri blinked, her eyes widening. "Kastner, Billy. He's the link. To all of this. Why did he rush down here after I called him? Surely, they have tons of cases all over the Bay Area and California. They could use their time better than…this. On a hunch. It has to be him." At this point, she was shaking his arm.

"Whoa, Bri, chill. This…is crazy." Trent's face betrayed deep concentration.

Bri stared up at him pleadingly. "Just think, Billy. Why did we follow all his commands blindly? We didn't need an undercover operation at the bistro. How did they know we had Chang as well? And Nadia? We told no one, except Meyers and Kastner. And I'm pretty sure Meyers wouldn't risk his sterling reputation over this!" Her voice reached a fevered pitch at that point, and Trent took her back to their car which was double-parked a few feet away.

"I trust you with my life, Bri, and I trust your skills as an inspector. I…"

"Then trust me now. We call his supervisor. If things check out, I drop it. If not…we have to go to Meyers with this evidence. Nadia…*everyone* could be in danger."

"What possible motive could he have?"

"That's what we need to pinpoint."

Trent still looked skeptical. "I dunno, Bri…"

"We'll make the call…what harm could it do?"

40

Korschev frowned at the man standing across from him. "I thought it was all arranged. You told me it was a certain thing. Now, I am left with a man trying to look after a woman who isn't really right in the head." He tapped his temple for emphasis.

On the whole, Korschev didn't trust the suited man. His badge may have given him some clout to begin with, but all the indecision and conveniently left out information was beginning to grate on him.

"I didn't know the investigation had proceeded to that point…"

Korschev's meaty fist hit the desk as he felt the vein bulge in his temple. "You should be more responsible. Now, there will be consequences."

"No, no, no consequences. I'll make it up to you. Where is the girl?"

* * *

The precinct was buzzing by the time Bri and Trent returned from the crime scene, having made sure Chang's body was on its way to the morgue. Pacing around their desks was Freedman. His head snapped up when he saw them.

"Hey, Kev, how's it hangin'?" Trent clapped him on the shoulder before rummaging around in his desk drawer for a treat.

"Inspectors, wow, I've been trying to get a hold of you both."

Bri took out her cell phone which, at that moment, pinged with the missed call. "Must've not been trying very hard."

"Yeah, yeah, sorry...uh...you remember that video footage you gave me? The grainy surveillance from the front of the station?"

Easing herself into her chair, Bri looked up at Freedman. "Yeah, I remember. We used it to see what happened to Max when he ran off that night." Her gut twisted and guilt blossomed anew. If only she'd chased after him...if only... Before the speculation fully set in, Bri was aware of Freedman's flapping hands and his mouth moving a mile a minute. She refocused.

"...so, I got curious, ya know? I wanted to see how far I could push the enhancement software and then I got a clear image. I fired it through the databases, and sure enough, I got a call from a guy at Interpol. They know who was watching Max that night."

"Well? Who is it?" Trent kicked his feet up on his side of the desk.

"Leon Skiliar. Recognize the name?" Freedman shoved his glasses up his nose, his head ping-ponging between both inspectors, waiting for them to provide the final puzzle piece to his mystery.

Trent rubbed his brow, and Bri nodded slowly. "Yes, we do know the name. He's the man who smuggled Max and Lina into the country. Agent Kastner told us."

"Hold on a sec...if you think Kastner is...ya know, why would he tell us the real name of the man who trafficked them? We always assumed it was an alias."

"Yeah, well, the guy from Interpol said they were monitoring flights, 'cause they know he sometimes uses his photo and with fake passports. He came into SFO about nine months ago under the name Demetri Saneslov."

Bri slapped her palm against the desk, causing both men to jump. "That dirty mother…"

"Language! There are children present." Trent jokingly gestured to Freedman, who scowled.

"This is getting really confusing. We need to make that call." Bri picked up the phone and began to dial. As she did, Meyers exited his office, obviously having heard the outburst and racket. He motioned for her to put it on speakerphone, and she complied.

"Agent Stephenson." The gruff voice answered after two rings.

"Yes, hi, this is Inspector Ryu with the SFPD. I was calling to ask about one of your agents here. His name is Kastner. We have a couple…"

"Damn it to hell."

"Pardon?" Meyers spoke up.

"Who's that?"

"Captain Bradley Meyers, Agent Stephenson. I'm here with Inspectors Ryu and Trent, the ones working in conjunction with your agent." Meyers' brow narrowed, a look he always had when he was concentrating too hard on something.

"Agent Kastner went AWOL, Captain. I've been trying to get a hold of him for a solid week. Said he got a call and had to take care of some family matters. Then, he never checked in."

Bri mouthed the word *fuck* in Trent's direction, and he frowned, both of them thinking the same thing—that Kastner was the reason Nadia and Chang had been attacked and killed, respectively.

"When did you last see him?"

"He rushed out of here yesterday morning, after speaking to you, right, Cap?"

Meyers' expression fell. "No...I was meeting with the superintendent yesterday morning."

"But he said he came from your office, sir..." Bri looked to Trent for verification, and her partner nodded his agreement.

Meyers maneuvered around the desks and moved into his office, without waiting to hear what Agent Stephenson had to say further on the matter.

"Inspectors, if you see him, arrest him. I'll be heading down there ASAP with my own agents. I'm sorry this has happened to you. We've known for a while he was a bit of a rogue, but we didn't know how far under he'd dug himself." The phone clicked, and Bri turned off speaker.

"Shit."

"Shit is an understatement, Bri. We need to notify our guys at the hospital, and then check out what was recovered from the raid on Sokolov's place. If Kastner is there, our entire case might be compromised. Text Cat. She deserves to have a heads up as well...and Ms. Vasquez." Trent shot her a pointed look, and Bri rubbed her aching temples.

"Yeah, I'll do that. In the meantime, I want to get Sokolov in for questioning. We're gonna have to tighten the screws, so to speak."

At that moment, Meyers made a beeline for them. "I'll echo your sentiments, Ryu. Shit. My files on the case are gone."

Bri found her feet. "That means he knows where Nadia is being held."

Trent was already pulling out his cell. "On it." Bri watched Meyers' knuckles whiten as he balled his hands into fists at the violation of their department's trust in Kastner. She felt much the same but waited with bated breath as Trent tried to contact their uniforms at the hospital.

"Hi, yeah, it's Trent. Don't let anyone in to see our wit. What? Get him the fuck out of there and hold him until we arrive." He jammed his finger at the screen. "Kastner just arrived at the hospital and was about to go in to see Nadia. They're detaining him until we get there."

Meyers held up a hand. "I've got this one. Why don't you two go see Dr. Hayes and find out what she dug up at the bistro? I have a few things I'd like to say to our friendly Fed. Then, you two can have at him."

Bri and Trent nodded, a half smile forming on Bri's lips. Maybe Meyers wasn't so by the book after all.

41
LINA

My head and arms hurt. We are in a run-down apartment across the street from where Leon was taking me. I'm sitting on a threadbare, stained couch as he paces in front of me. I don't ask questions as to why we are here. He is unnerved, even I recognize the signs of someone on the edge. He has been on the phone to Korschev, alternating between English and Russian. I pick up the words, "rat" and "police." My heart lightens, then falls. If I am taken by the police, what will happen to Max?

"Eyes down!" he barks at me, needing a vent for all the panic I know is building inside him.

You could hit him. He's unarmed. Better yet, let me do it. Please, little Lina.

"Shush!"

Leon's hands are around my throat in an instant, and spots dance in front of my eyes. "What did you say?"

"I..." My tongue fills my mouth. My brain is deprived of oxygen. Something will break in my throat soon.

He releases me, and I fall forward, sputtering, coughing.

"You're lucky Mr. Korschev wants you alive. He's getting a lot of money for you, but fuck knows for what. A saggy pussy?" Leon laughs. "How many times have you been fucked now, Lina?"

My throat burns. I want to retort, but I say nothing, eyes down. Behave.

He got you here, Lina. It is his fault we are here.

"Answer me!" He backhands me. He won't really hurt me. Korschev won't stand for any real damage to his merchandise.

A whimper escapes my lips, the only sign of weakness I allow.

"Pathetic. You were easy prey."

The voice inside me is threatening to unleash. I am the only thing holding him back. I must stay alive. For Max.

Leon looks out the window. "Fuck." He pulls out his cell phone again. "Boss, they have Sokolov."

I hear the muffled shouts of an angry man. In all my time here, I have done my best not to anger him, not to anger anyone. Women who have angered them get punished. I have been good.

Yes, letting them rape you is so good.

Stop it! I cover my ears and grit my teeth to prevent myself from actually voicing the words.

Leon is looking at me. I can feel his icy stare. "Yes, she's fine. You sure about this, boss? She's not exactly stable…" His words are cut off by more muffled yelling. "Yeah, yeah, sorry, sir. I'll wait here." He hangs up. "I'm sure he won't mind if we have some fun, *mudishka*."

His hand tangles in my hair, yanking painfully. I go numb.

42

"You two took your time. I thought you'd have been here hours ago." Hayes peered at them over the rim of her coffee mug.

Bri shrugged. "We had something we needed to take care of first."

Trent flopped into one of the chairs in front of Hayes' desk, propping his booted feet up on the surface, body slouched. "Yeah, Kastner is a rat."

Grumbling at the possible breech in protocol, Bri swatted at his feet so she could get past him. "We don't know that yet."

"He did seem…odd to me," Hayes remarked as she set the mug aside. "Twitchy."

"Twitchy? Is that a technical term?" Trent shot her one of his trademark grins.

"Quiet you. So, what's the deal with him?"

"We don't know yet. He was detained at St. Francis trying to speak to our assault victim. His supervisor says he's been AWOL."

"Mysterious." Hayes wiggled her fingers then resecured her bun, methodically replacing the bobby pins. "So, the Little Russian Tea House…"

"Room."

"Yes." Hayes shot her a look, and Bri clamped her lips shut. "Not so little, as it turns out. He's renovated it to include an underground storage facility for alcohol and dry goods. We had a helluva time combing through it all. Still, I found something you're going to love." She pulled out a couple of sheets of paper.

Bri skimmed the report. "Broken glass?"

"Yup. One of my techs pieced it together, and we found it was part of a Stoli Elit bottle. Thanks to its unique composition, we were able to compare it to the sample we pulled from Max's stomach."

"And?"

"It was a match. I can assure you, Sokolov was none-too-pleased when he saw us seizing his entire stock. Hand blown glass bottles and they come with a solid gold ice pick. Retails for…"

"$3,000 a bottle. Yes, he made a great show of telling us that."

"Who the hell pays that much for vodka?" Trent locked his fingers behind his head, jiggling his leg. "Gimme a bottle of Bud any day."

"People with too much money and not enough ways to spend it." Bri turned back to Hayes. "So…we have him on that alone?"

"I'd say at least on the charge of concealing evidence. If he knew about the murder beforehand, he could go down as an accessory. But you guys'll have to talk to the DA, I guess." Hayes tapped the papers together in a neat stack, setting them in one of the plastic trays on her desk. "Be an even stronger case if we could have found the heroin or even the needle used."

"Accessory after the fact, Bri. We'd nail him on that." Trent rocked to his feet, ever the optimist. "I'll get on the horn to Central and see about an arrest warrant. Gonna have to play this one close to the chest, especially since we don't know what Kastner has done." He made a face and pulled out his cell, wandering out of the office.

Hayes angled her head, waiting until he was out of earshot, before fixing Bri with a Cheshire Cat grin. "Soooo?"

Bri blinked a few times. "Soooo, what?"

"Come on, I'm not blind. I make my living picking out things people miss. Still, you'd have to be blind not to see you're floating, but distressed."

"Floating and distressed. Is that an official diagnosis, Doc?"

Hayes pouted. "Come on. Don't make me beg. Give me something…"

Bri was reluctant to let Hayes in on her spur of the moment rendezvous with Petra. Both were walking a fine line, but since Nadia wouldn't be testifying against a dead man, Bri caved to pressure. Who knew, it might be cathartic.

"Trent, the worm, gave Petra my address."

"Petra…Vasquez? The woman who runs the charity…"

"Haven. For survivors of human trafficking. Yes, her." Bri twisted her dark ponytail around her finger, twirling it around the hairband before letting it fall. She could feel her heart speed up at the thought of that night, and the thought of how much she wanted to tell Petra everything they'd uncovered. Still, she knew there would be time enough for that.

"And?" Hayes swirled her hand in the air. "What now? Was it a fling? Love at first sight?"

"I…we…don't know." Apprehension suddenly flooded Bri's chest, causing a lump to form in her throat. "You know things never work out with anyone for me. I'm such a walking law enforcement cliché. Married to the job and all that crap."

Hayes stood, circling the desk and sitting next to her.

"You can't say that. Those people before weren't right for you. They didn't get it. It's like my ex. He didn't get it. Too needy."

"But are we always doomed to be that? Unless you're in this line of work, you're never going to really get it. I don't know how people do it."

"What did your dad do? He and your mom seem pretty happy."

"I guess it was a different era." Bri shifted in her chair.

Hayes worried her lower lip between her teeth. "There's nothing saying you have to jump in with both feet. Get a feel for the water. Also, it seems like she does know the business. If anything, her life might be more complicated and stressful than yours."

Always blunt and to the point, Bri knew she could count on Hayes to keep things in perspective. Perhaps she was overthinking everything. However, the security she had felt when she woke up next to Petra was something she hadn't experienced in a long time.

Trent ambled back into the room. "So, the warrant is being processed. We can pick it up and head over to arrest Sokolov. Interpol would apparently like to speak to him as well. This is probably going to go Federal, but we get jurisdiction for the accessory after the fact."

Hayes nodded. "That is good to hear. I'll let you guys get going." She touched Bri's shoulder, giving it a squeeze. "Roll with things. If it doesn't work out, it doesn't work out. You'll be richer for the experience."

"Listen to this relationship guru. When was your last date, Hayes?"

She narrowed her eyes. "When was *yours*? Or has the lovely Christine still got you by the balls?"

Trent opened his mouth to retort, but the words failed to come, and he reddened instead. The barbs were always good natured, and both knew there was no real malice behind them.

Bri laughed. "Okay, okay, we're professionals, remember?"

Resting her hands on the arms of the chair, Hayes stood. "Right, right. Okay, after all this wraps up, we're having drinks."

"It's a date."

43
LINA

I begin to count in my head, like I do all the other times my body is being used. The voice screams, unbearable. I want to claw at my scalp, but my face is pressed into the mattress. It smells of stale body sweat. My arms are restrained painfully behind my back.

Now, Lina. We can get Max later… Let me in!

Tears slip unchecked down my cheeks. Dare I? I jam my eyes closed, and my mind goes blank.

✷ ✷ ✷

Little Lina…time to wake up.

The voice taunts me, and I'm lying on my back on the bed. I blink, coming back to reality. My hands and arms sting. I lift them above my head and see the deep scratches along my pale flesh, the already forming bruises and abrasions. I shiver, realizing I am still naked. Sitting up, the blood rushes from my head and I groan.

Turn around, Little Lina.

"No."

Do it! The voice is harsher than before, almost gleeful

though, as if bragging about a conquest.

I turn my body, taking in the jeans bunched at Leon's ankles. He's wearing Nike sneakers and I spend an unusually long amount of time studying the swoosh on the side. Max wanted a pair so badly back in Ukraine. I move my gaze further up, waiting for the inevitable moment he drags me down again, but his legs are still, penis flaccid against his thigh.

His stomach is partially exposed, t-shirt raised slightly. His chest is still.

"No, what did you do?"

Laughter inside my head. No answer.

I get to my knees and look at his face, eyes wide, tongue purple. His neck is red and angry looking. He's not breathing. Not moving. Dead. This takes a moment to register, and then I fly off the bed, my back painfully hitting the wall.

"What did you do?!" I shout again, grabbing for my clothes, clutching them to my body.

What you couldn't do, Lina. What you wanted to do. Now, get dressed and go outside. Run.

I blindly obey.

44

Kastner walked with purpose into the hospital, flashing his badge at the desk. He knew what he had to do. A cold sweat pricked his neck. He did not deserve his namesake. When he joined the FBI, he had taken an oath. Muttering to himself, he repeated the words as he walked.

"I, Robert Kastner, do solemnly swear that I will support and defend the Constitution of the United States against all enemies, foreign and domestic; that I will bear true faith and allegiance to the same; that I take this obligation freely, without any mental reservation or purpose of evasion; and that I will well and faithfully discharge the duties of the office on which I am about to enter. So help me God…"

He had failed wholly to uphold any element of the oath. The minute he had signed his good name away to Korschev, he was ruined. They had trapped him so seamlessly, he didn't even know it had happened, until after it had happened. Korschev had promised to keep his secret, as long as he did as requested.

As soon as Inspector Ryu had called the office, he'd left without so much as a word to his supervisor. This was it. This was his endgame. He'd play the cards and do this final thing for the Mafia. Then, he would place his duty weapon between his teeth, and end it. It wasn't worth living in such shame and disgrace. Law enforcement were not well received in jails or prisons.

"...I will support and defend the Constitution of the United States against all enemies, foreign and domestic..." He slipped the weapon from his shoulder holster as he approached the hospital room door.

"Agent Robert Kastner...place the weapon on the ground and put your hands behind your head. You're under arrest."

His vision blurred.

* * *

Petra sat by Nadia's bedside, tears forming in her eyes. She shuddered to think what would have happened had Bri and Inspector Trent not discovered the duplicitous nature of Agent Kastner. The man sat outside the room, head bowed, hands cuffed. There was a pathetic aura about him, but Petra shook off any empathy she might have felt for him. He had lied to all of them, had plotted to dispose of Nadia. Did he even know about the poor little boy who had been killed by the Mafia?

Nadia's eyes fluttered in sleep, blissfully unaware of the events taking place around her. Petra was thankful for that. However, she wasn't safe here anymore. The guilt was heavy in her heart, compounded with the worry for the other young women in her care. She reminded herself to ask Bri if the location of her shelter had been revealed. A tear trickled down her cheek, and she brushed it away. What chaos her life had been thrown into, all for agreeing to help find out something about the murdered boy.

She remembered that day, which felt so long ago in her mind, but was really just a week or so ago. Seeing Bri and Inspector Trent enter the Starbucks, looking at the pale face of the boy on a cold autopsy table...seeing the pleading behind Bri's eyes. Was it that which had made her decide to help…or had it been her own budding attraction rearing its head?

Petra knew she had crossed that fine line, showing up at Bri's door. She knew it as soon as the words left her lips asking Trent for her address. Still, he hadn't been forced to give it to her either. She sensed the comradery between the partners, the 'got your back' type. She knew he wouldn't have done anything to compromise her—maybe even thinking it was for her own good.

Nadia stirred, opening her eyes. "Ms. Vasquez? Are you okay?" Her sleepy face could hardly conceal her concern.

"Yes, I'm fine, my dear. I am…relieved, mostly." She squeezed her hand. "You are looking well. The doctors are pleased with your progress. As am I."

Frowning, Nadia's eyes traced over her face. She could feel their path, as if she was touching her. "There's more."

"Yes. The man who attacked you is dead. However, you're not out of danger yet… I'm sorry, Nadia, but you must leave the city. I wish there was another way."

Taking Petra's hand between the pair of hers, Nadia smiled. "I knew I would have to, someday. I had hoped it wouldn't be so soon…"

"There are dangerous men after you." Petra didn't elaborate, knowing a survivor's trust in law enforcement was already tenuous. To hear that they had been betrayed by a member of the FBI would likely set Nadia back in her recovery, and she had come so far already.

"What will happen?"

"There have been arrangements made with the US Marshals to take you to a safe house and then from there, you will receive a new identity. You must not…contact me." Petra's voice hitched, and she covered her mouth with her free hand, taking a moment to regain composure. "I'm so sorry."

This unexpected influx of emotion threw Petra off guard. She was stronger than this, better than this.

"Ms. Vasquez, you gave me my life back. Without you, I wouldn't be where I was today. I can start afresh, and I will be happy. I promised myself that the moment I knew I was going to survive. Please don't cry. Maybe…one day…we will meet again."

Standing, Petra gently embraced the young woman, in awe at her strength which seemed to surpass that of someone so young. Still, when you'd been through the horrors they both had seen, maturity came quickly.

"Goodbye, Nadia. I am, and always will be, proud of you."

With a final teary smile, Petra departed.

45

The rain, which had been threatening to fall for the entire day, finally broke through the angry clouds hanging over the city, as Bri and Trent wove through traffic to get to the Little Russian Tea Room. The revelations about Kastner and the link to Max's murder laid heavily on Bri's mind. Why would Kastner betray his badge over this? When they'd first met, he had been so confident, so sure of his position in helping the victims of human trafficking. Now, she wondered how many were in that position because of his behind-the-scenes actions. Her hands tightened on the steering wheel, knuckles white.

"What is it?" Trent broke through her thoughts.

"Kastner. Why would he do this?"

"I hope we get a chance to ask him. Meyers says they've just brought him in and are holding him until his supervisor can get there. We've been asked to wait before questioning him, but I think the FBI have given us a courtesy in letting us do that."

"Yeah, they didn't have to do that. They could have hauled him off to some secret prison, and we'd never find out the reasons."

Trent jabbed his finger on the window defroster as

the wipers swished in methodical rhythm, filling the silence which lapsed between them. The splash of the tires through the puddles on the streets soon added to the swishing, and calm descended around Bri as they drew closer. She maneuvered the car behind the flashing lights of the patrol cars.

Stepping out onto the wet pavement, Bri pulled the hood of her all-weather jacket up, glad she'd had the foresight to grab it this morning instead of the leather one. Her thoughts returned to Petra, hoping she had had her chance to say goodbye to Nadia before Witness Protection took over. She hung back, considering texting her, but decided it should wait.

As they neared the entrance to the building, Sokolov was emerging in cuffs. The uniforms had been given orders to remove him quickly into Trent and Bri's custody for interrogation at the station, at which point Meyers would turn him over to Interpol for further questioning. Trent gripped Sokolov's arm and recited the Miranda warning. The man looked close to blubbering, his face ruddy, the gel in his hair dissipating in the rain leaving dark worm-like strands over his forehead. He met Bri's eyes and recognition dawned momentarily. As he was hustled into the back of a patrol car, one of the uniforms gasped, pointing her finger to the front of the building opposite.

Bri glanced over and her heart dropped to her knees. She blinked a few times, clearing her vision. "Holy shit…"

Trent slammed the patrol car door shut, brow furrowed. "What?"

"Look." Bri indicated in the same direction as the officer. Then, as if the world had sped up again, she sprang into action. "Get paramedics en route ASAP. Trent, grab the blanket from the trunk."

Trent finally turned his head, and echoed Bri's

sentiments. "Holy shit…" He raced to the trunk.

With the street blocked off, Bri crossed it with ease, cautiously approaching the slim, young woman standing frozen in place on the sidewalk. She was wearing a thin jacket, jeans, and new sneakers, the rain rapidly soaking through the insufficient layers of clothing.

"Lina?"

The blue eyes snapped open, petrified. She stepped backwards, her flight-or-fight reflex sparking into action.

"Lina, please. I'm Inspector Briana Ryu…I've been investigating your case. Your brother…"

"Max?" She brushed aside long, ropey strands of blonde hair.

Trent jogged to Bri's side, startling the young woman. He noted the reaction and swiftly handed Bri the blanket, moving away. Bri kept her attention fixated on Lina.

"My partner, Inspector Billy Trent. He won't hurt you. Please, will you come with us, Lina?" She opened the blanket, holding it out for the trembling girl.

Hesitating, eyes darting between all the officers present and the two inspectors, Lina finally collapsed into Bri's arms, heaving sobs racking her abused body. Bri wrapped the blanket around her and held her, allowing her those moments of comfort which had been no doubt denied to her over so many months. "You're safe now." She made sure to only touch the blanket. The ordeal wasn't over for Lina yet, and she would have to go through an examination once they got her to the hospital. Bri didn't want to contaminate any evidence.

Through the cries, Lina spoke softly. "He killed him."

Bri shot a look over her shoulder to Trent, extending her arms out to peer into Lina's face. "Who, Lina?"

"Leon. Upstairs."

The sirens from the ambulance blared as it parked alongside the curb.

"Trent, can you take two uniforms? I'll go with Lina

to the hospital." She guided Lina to the open back doors of the ambulance.

"He killed him. He said it was for the best."

Bri frowned, watching Trent mobilize the officers and enter the building, weapons drawn. "Who said it?"

"The voice. It was my only chance." Lina began to cry again, drawing in gasping breaths of air. The female paramedic gently placed her on a gurney, but as soon as Lina saw the male one, she began to scream and fight.

Bri quickly jumped into the back of the rig, ordering the male out. "She's terrified. Just drive." She placed a comforting hand on Lina's arm. "He's here to help. We all are. Shh."

Lina gripped her hand with great force, more than Bri thought the emaciated girl was possible of expelling. "My brother. Where is he?"

The female paramedic swung the doors shut, as she set about taking Lina's vitals and attaching an IV bag of fluids.

Bri squeezed back, recognizing the need for kind human contact. "Rest now. There will be answers soon enough. I promise." She didn't have the heart to tell her in that moment that Max was dead. Maybe Petra would have a kinder way. *A kinder way.* There was no kind way of telling a traumatized victim that their only family was dead.

Lina's eyes fluttered closed, and her breathing evened.

"I gave her a mild sedative, Inspector."

Bri felt the grip loosen on her hand and tears stung her eyes. "Thanks."

The lulling sound of wipers and tires through water melded with the sirens. Bri took the time to remove her cell phone from her pocket and texted Petra.

We have Lina. St. Francis en route. Can you meet us there?

It didn't take long for the reply: *I'm already here.*

※ ※ ※

Doctors were already on standby when the ambulance screamed into the designated parking spot at the back of the hospital. The doors snapped open, and Bri waited while the gurney was unloaded, following behind. She tugged on the arm of one of the doctors, an elderly man with tanned skin and white hair. "Human trafficking victim, severe sexual violence and mental trauma. Please…let me go with her."

The doctor hesitated and then nodded. "We'll make sure she's stable and then get an examination organized."

"Wait until she wakes up. Consent has been taken away from her for so long…" Bri watched the gurney heading off and she jogged to catch up, alongside the doctor. "Please…"

The white-haired doctor nodded sympathetically. "I'll make a note on her records."

"And women only. Please."

The doctor paused, holding Bri back. "Inspector, are you okay?"

Watching as the medical team moved into a curtained bay, Bri took a moment to speak to the man. "It never ceases to shock me what human beings are capable of doing to each other."

He nodded in response. "Yes, but it's what we can do for her that will make the difference." He guided Bri toward the bay.

"There's a woman, Petra Vasquez. She's with the Haven charity for victims of human trafficking. She'll be here… Also, I need to call for protective detail for Lina…"

"I'm already here." Petra's soothing voice met Bri's ears, as the doctor smiled and continued through the curtain.

Bri revolved, taking in Petra's reddened eyes. "Nadia?"

"Already on her way to a safe place."

Ignoring all the protocol and every objection her mind threw at her, Bri embraced Petra, nestling her head on the other woman's shoulder. Her eyes squeezed shut, fighting tears.

Petra gripped Bri tightly. "You did well, Bri."

"It was luck. She appeared across the street from the Tea Room." Bri's voice was muffled against Petra's neck.

"How did she get there?"

"I don't know, but she said 'he' killed him—a voice." Lifting her head, she looked into Petra's eyes. "What does that mean?"

"I'm sure we'll find out soon enough." Petra cupped her cheek. "Oh, Bri…"

Bri placed her hand over Petra's, pressing the cool palm into her warm flesh. "Just a little longer. I have a few things to wrap up and then we can talk, okay?"

Petra smiled, running her thumb over Bri's cheekbone before letting her hand drop.

"I have to go back to the station, meet Trent and find out what he discovered from the room Lina was in. Can you be her advocate here? I trust you."

Petra trailed her hands down Bri's arms, taking her hands in her own. "Yes, I will make sure she is safe until we can find out more about what has happened."

Bri smiled, relieved. "Thank you." Reluctantly releasing Petra's hands, she turned to leave. The moment of intimacy had driven new vigor into Bri's heart, giving her the energy she needed to carry on to the end of the investigation. There were unanswered questions, and she wasn't going to rest until every loose end had been tied up—starting with Kastner and Sokolov.

46

Andrei Korschev shoved papers into a trash can before setting them alight. All his girls had been moved out rapidly, as soon as he had heard Sokolov was going to be arrested. The fat man would sing like a bird. He tried Leon's cell phone one more time, hurling his against the wall when Leon's voicemail parroted into his ear yet again.

Gathering a forged passport out of the drawer, he collected the remaining money from the safe. The Feds wouldn't find him, or his girls, and he could always get new stock anyway. Everyone was disposable. His hand brushed against a black and white photograph of Inspector Briana Ryu.

He rattled off a string of swear words in Russian, tearing the photograph to shreds. He was not a man who would let a slight against him go by without retribution. Gathering the last of his documents, he shut the office door and turned to one of his goons.

"Burn the place down."

❋ ❋ ❋

Texting Trent on her walk out from the emergency room,

Bri was happy to see him drive up, completely ignoring the fact he didn't even move to let her take over. Anyway, she didn't think she could drive at this point, so was happy to let him have his moment. As soon as they were en route back to the Central station, she asked the question that had been lingering in her mind.

"What happened in the building?"

Trent turned a corner. "We found a man dead in the bed. His ID pegged him as Leon Skiliar."

"And? Any other men around?"

"No. The techs are on it, and Cat arrived just as I was leaving. Bri…there were signs of sexual activity, and it looked like he'd been strangled."

"Shit." Bri shook her head. "I hope to hell we can get whoever did it…and thank them."

"Well, that's the thing. There were no signs of anyone else having been in the room. I mean, we'll know more when the evidence comes back, and Cat gives us the COD." Trent steered into the parking spot in front of the station. "Are you sure she said 'he'?"

"Positive."

"Huh. Strange." The pair got out of the car and walked into the precinct. "Well, I guess first things first. Sokolov or Kastner?"

Meyers interrupted as he met them at the door. "Kastner has been taken into custody by the FBI. They'll feed back any information relevant to us."

"Shit. Why the change of heart?" Bri was furious. She had wanted to ask him why he had used them in such a deplorable way.

"Sorry, Inspector, I wish I knew."

"And Sokolov?"

"Interrogation room 2."

By the time she entered the windowless cubicle, Bri's temper had boiled to an extreme she would often try to curb if under any other circumstance. However, by all outward appearances, she was deathly calm. Trent shot her a sidelong glance—he knew her mood instantly.

The man before them was sweating profusely, his face melancholic and despondent. Desperation shone in his glassy eyes as his head jerked up upon their arrival. Bri stared him down, trying to get a measure of the man who knowingly protected people who treated women like chattel. The silence in the room was only punctuated by the man's labored breathing. Bri's throat closed at the smell of his aftershave—an overpriced, overvalued brand which lingered heavily in the air.

"Interview commencing at 1600 hours, Inspectors William Trent and Briana Ryu present with Vasily Sokolov." Trent began the recording. His eyes flicked up to Sokolov. "Can we confirm you have signed denying a right to retain counsel, Mr. Sokolov?"

Bri was surprised a man with such connections would risk such exposure. Then again, if he did squeal, he would find himself at the end of cushy deal with the DA, and probably the US Attorney.

"Yes, I have."

"And you do this of sound mind, and without any coercion?"

Bri hid her smile. Trent was an expert at interrogation. No way was he going to let anything slide as inadmissible when this came to court.

"Yes, I do. You have the paper."

Trent nodded, withdrawing it from the file and skimming it over. "Mr. Sokolov, you understand you have been arrested on suspicion of being in violation of Penal Code 236.1, relating to human trafficking in the State of California. Do you have anything to say about this?"

Sokolov straightened, bursting out with defenses, not considering his words. "I was never directly involved with the girls! I only hid money, ran drugs, that type of thing." Once he realized what he had said, Bri watched his face turn even more crimson. She inwardly smiled again.

"We have crime scene technicians combing your restaurant and home as we speak, Mr. Sokolov. Any further charges will be defined as we gather evidence. Tell me...do you know the whereabouts of an Andrei Korschev?"

"Korschev...yes, he is the one who trafficked the girls into the country. He asked me to hide that one...the one who was to be sold. I told him I wanted nothing to do with the girls. They were his business, but he threatened my family." Sokolov's hands were visibly sweating, the gold rings on his fingers glinting in the fluorescent lighting of the interrogation suite.

"Why didn't you come to the police, Mr. Sokolov?" Bri was dying to hear his response to this. "If you knew illegal activity was taking place, wouldn't you report it, as a good citizen?"

"You don't understand." His eyes fixed on Bri. "They have a great reach. If they didn't get me, the Triads would. I need protection. I will speak, but I want safety for myself and my family."

"That's something you'll have to discuss with the district attorney. Can you tell us anything about this boy?"

Trent withdrew the picture of Max, the one taken while he had lain cold on the autopsy table. Bri dug her nails into her hand. The ordeal still pained her—to think she had let him slip away into the night.

"Yes, I do."

"And how do you know him?" Trent pressed, edging the photograph closer with a fingertip.

Sokolov recoiled. "He...came in with one of Korschev's men. They went down to the cellar... Next thing I know, he is coming back without the boy. He says not to look in my freezer, and then he comes back two days later with another man and they leave out the back door."

"He was a child, that boy." Bri gritted her teeth, unable to keep quiet about the callousness in which this scum of a human described the death.

"That is the thing. I never knew. I never knew the boy was harmed!" Sokolov's voice rose an octave.

Bri retorted, "You never thought to look, Mr. Sokolov. Not only are you an accessory to human trafficking, but to murder as well."

"I...I change my mind. I want an attorney. Now. I need protection for my family." He cradled his face in his hands.

Trent sighed. "Interview suspended at 1645 hours." He exited the room and motioned to the officers outside. "Take him back to the holding cell."

Bri meekly followed, feeling like she'd just blown their chance to get answers. Trent placed a hand on her shoulder. "We knew he'd eventually see that an attorney is the way to go. I get your anger, Bri, I really do." She smiled, taking it in the comforting way it was meant.

"We should go see Hayes and get an idea of what's happening on her end of things."

Trent nodded. "I'll give her a call and check out where she's at." Before he could dial, he tilted his head. "You okay, Ryu?"

Bri smiled, watching the officers lead Sokolov out of the interrogation room in cuffs, the man blubbering softly. "I will be. Once we know for sure Lina is safe. I still don't know how the hell we're gonna tell her about Max..."

"Let Petra do it."

The tone in Trent's voice had Bri tilting her head with curiosity. "You..."

"You're kinda obvious, Ryu. Don't fuck it up. I kinda like her." Trent lifted the phone to his ear and sauntered off to the row of desks.

Bri shook her head with a laugh. "I'll get the

car…jerk."

Trent waved a hand absently as she spun and headed out to the garage.

47

"That girl has *cojones*, I'll say that much." Hayes balled and chucked her rubber gloves into the trash, as she met Trent and Bri in the corridor outside the autopsy room.

"Why, what's up?" Bri had her hands in the pockets of her hoodie, clenching and unclenching her fists methodically. Her stress levels had continued to rise after they had received word—just as they were leaving—that Korschev had fled, whereabouts unknown. There would never be peace for Lina as long as he was on the loose.

Hayes jerked her head. "Come into my office…"

"Said the spider to the fly…" Trent finished with a flair. He could no doubt feel the tension emanating from Bri and was trying to break it. It was an admirable effort.

The inspectors took their customary places opposite Hayes, who pulled out the USB with her digitally recorded notes for later transcription, "You already know some of my preliminary observations. However, I found something exceptional while examining the body."

"Does the initial identity match?" Bri piped up, wanting confirmation that one of Lina's torturers had been eliminated. She wasn't ashamed of the joy she felt at this prospect.

213

"His wallet confirmed his identity." Hayes furrowed her brow. "There was no disturbance of his personal effects, according to the techs."

"Okay, so, what's the situation with the body?" Trent returned them to the task at hand.

Hayes' frown deepened. "The marks around his neck were exerted with an unusual amount of force—not something I'd expect from a woman...especially one who was in such a weakened state. However, the bruising around his neck is extensive. The blood vessels burst with the pressure, yet the remaining handprints indicate a smaller palm size."

"So...wait. You're saying it was a woman who did this? How do you know?" Bri was reluctant to believe Lina had done such a thing, but all the evidence did fall into place. She needed the confirmation of that fact.

"Yes, I would say so. Besides, there was no evidence of anyone else in the room. We'll know more once we do a kit on Lina and compare the fluid results to those we found on the body."

Bri clenched her teeth together. "Another violation of her body."

"But we have to know for certain, Bri. We're not doing this to be cruel." Hayes stood, leaning against the desk in front of her. "We need to build a picture of what happened. Under the circumstances, she wouldn't be charged, I'm certain. Self-defense..."

"We're just making the victim into the offender again. How many human trafficking victims have been charged with crimes which are certainly beyond their own fault? Prostitution, deportation..." Bri began to rattle off the list of facts she had read about online. She thought of Petra, fighting desperately for the rights of the girls in her care. "Doesn't seem right, does it?" She lifted her chin, hating the feeling of tears stinging her eyes.

"No, it certainly doesn't." Trent leaned back in his

chair. "We'll need to go interview Lina in the hospital. Do you want to call Petra and see what the situation is like?"

Bri fumbled for her cell phone. "Yeah, I will." She was angry at the tremor in her hand—a result of the rage bubbling inside her at this injustice.

"Bri, it's not certain. We need to conduct the investigation...although, I think with your closeness to the situation..."

Bri leapt to her feet. "Are you questioning my impartiality to the situation? Cause I damned well hope that's not what you're even thinking, Trent."

Hayes rocked forward, holding out her hands. "Whoa, Bri, we get it. You know we have jobs to do. Our personal feelings never come into play. We'll do all we can to show it was self-defense—for Lina's sake."

The irrational reaction made Bri flush with shame. "I'm sorry. I really am."

Trent shook his head, standing as well. "No sweat. We all feel the same inside. It's why we work well together. You're not afraid to speak what's on your mind, and yeah, I get it. You're upset and want to see this through to the end. I don't think the Cap'll object either. We'll make it work, Bri." He wrapped her in a tight, one-armed hug. "This has taken a toll. I'd say go home, but I know you wouldn't listen. So, let's go see Petra and Lina. Get some answers, 'kay?"

Bri hated feeling weak, but for the moment, she let herself lean on her two closest friends, Hayes' hand rubbing her back. "'Kay."

"And after this clusterfuck is over, we're gonna grab a few beers and chill, like we said before. Cool?" Trent angled back, looking down at her.

"Cool."

※ ※ ※

Petra sat by Lina's bedside, eyes occasionally lifting to the sleeping girl. Her face was tense, even in the enveloping arms of Morpheus. The doctor had prescribed a sedative, concerned about the numbness in which the young woman had endured all the examinations. They had sought her consent, yet the only signs of life were the sharp squeezes she gave Petra's hand. She hoped this would be the last time Lina would ever experience this upon her person. It was a necessary evil.

Antibiotics ran from the IV into her thin hand. Petra observed the scratch marks on the backs of them—some deep gouges. Were they inflicted by the man Bri had told her had been found in the place where Lina was being held? Had she truly killed him? Lina had not spoken since they brought her in. She merely stared blankly. Petra had seen it before—disassociation. It was easier to withdraw into the mind than face the brutal trauma she had experienced. Sometimes, the victim developed other personalities, more equipped with facing the pain.

A soft moan escaped Lina's lips, drawing Petra's instant focus. She began thrashing on the bed. With practiced ease, Petra rose and pressed the button to call the nurse. She murmured soothing words to the distressed girl until the nurse arrived and was able to give some medicinal relief. Lina soon calmed.

"I don't know how anyone could endure what she has," the nurse remarked in hushed tones to Petra.

"People are programmed to survive if they know they have something to live for. The endurance of the human spirit is remarkable. It takes a lot to see it broken." Her heart sank, knowing she would soon have to comfort Lina when she was told about Max. Inwardly, she wondered if it would break her, but she refused to accept the young woman couldn't be helped.

The nurse nodded solemnly and left the room; Petra resumed her vigil, only again to be distracted by a quiet knock on the door. It opened, and Bri and Inspector

Trent entered silently. She stood and approached Bri, hesitating as she glanced to Trent. In this case, it was Bri who instigated any form of intimacy. She hugged her, and Petra felt the despair in the usually steadfast woman. Trent nodded politely once the hug was broken.

"How is she doing?" Bri asked softly.

"Some distress, but they did sedate her. What news is there of the man who was found?"

Trent tried to smile, give some sign of sympathy, but failed. "We think Lina strangled him. We don't know how, though. Our coroner says that she exerted a considerable amount of force on the man's neck."

"Will she be charged?"

"Not if we can help it," Bri responded vehemently. "She's a victim of some fucked up people. I'll be damned if I see her go to prison for her actions."

Petra took Bri's trembling hand in hers and squeezed it gently. "We will make sure of it."

"And the doctors? What are they saying?" Trent was trying to get a picture of the situation, and Petra didn't begrudge him his need to investigate and get answers.

"Severe internal trauma. She may need surgery at a later point. They are running blood tests on her to check for any STIs but have started her on an antibiotic cocktail as a precaution. Her body…is so battered and emaciated. They are giving her fluids as well." Petra's voice broke, and she steadied herself, trying to maintain composure.

"We'll need to interview her…you know that." Trent continued to speak, but Petra's focus had shifted to Bri, who was looking at the girl dwarfed by the crisp hospital sheets and gown.

She turned her chin upward to Bri's partner. "Yes, I know. But we must be careful. I fear she may be mentally unstable. We'll know more when she wakes, I imagine."

"You have a place for her?" Bri asked, keeping her eyes on Lina.

"We will make a place. She is important to you, and therefore, important to me." Petra had kept her hand in Bri's, knowing how the touch would provide comfort to her unsettled soul. A blossoming of emotion budded in her chest for the woman beside her, something she had not expected to feel again.

A flicker of a smile passed over Bri's lips. "Thanks. We should go. You'll call when she wakes up?"

"Of course."

Petra watched the pair go. It would be a long road, but she hoped Lina would be able to weather it.

48
LINA

I sit on my bed in the room at the shelter, and the same numbness I had felt when I first found out Leon had tricked me into coming to California engulfs me. All the lies and deceit have compounded in my mind. Max is dead—the person I have fought so hard to survive for no longer exists in this world. They killed him, killed him for trying to help me.

The single tear burns its way down my cold cheek, the first truly anguished tear I have cried in many months. I have been abused, tortured, treated like I am not a person—a thing to be used and discarded like a piece of trash. There was so much I had wanted to do, but nothing feels worthwhile anymore. Inspector Ryu assures me there will be no charges filed against me in Leon's death. In truth, I do not remember killing him. I don't know what gave me the power to do so, but the voice has faded. Everyone has been so kind, but I am completely alone now, and Korschev is still out there.

Go on, Little Lina. Go on. Make the pain vanish.

My hand trembles as I extract the blades from my

pocket. God will forgive me.

The red line of blood blossoms, and the world fuzzes away before my eyes. I am free.

49

Bri's phone blared to life as she rolled over in bed with a groan. For the first time in a few weeks, she had actually managed to have a dreamless sleep. Petra's number lit up the screen. She answered and then checked the time. Two am. "Hello?"

"Briana…" Petra's voice was breathless, panicked.

Sitting up, Bri's heart began to race, tossing aside formalities. "Petra, what is it? Breathe."

"Lina…she…she… We try to prevent these things. We know how vulnerable survivors are. I don't know how… We do bed checks, but she got hold of a razor…broke it…" Fresh sobs filled Bri's ear, her blood leaden in her veins.

"Petra…I have to call this in."

"No, no, please. My girls would be compromised, they would…" Her voice broke with choking cries.

"Okay, okay…I'll need one…one person to come with me. Not Inspector Trent. The medical examiner. Do you trust me?"

"Yes, of course. Please, no sirens. No lights. I'll text you the address."

Bri hung up the phone and immediately called Hayes,

221

who picked up on the second ring, saying she would be over as soon as she could.

The shelter was truly nondescript. Anyone would have mistaken it for an office building or apartment complex. Petra met them outside, quickly ushering them to Lina's room.

"I tried to save her…but she…was dead when I found her." The sobs started afresh.

Hayes' expression was grim as she performed the checks on Lina. "I can't say for sure without autopsy, but body temperature would indicate she died around midnight. Her body is just entering rigor." She rocked back on her heels. "I need to get a team in here, Bri." She shifted her eyes to Petra. "You know protocol. I cannot…" Hayes glanced to Bri, pleading with her eyes.

Petra was hesitating, and Bri sensed it. "We'll be as careful as we can. No sirens. I promise. Your girls won't be compromised."

Petra wrung her hands, fisting them in her sweater. "Okay."

Hayes smiled reassuringly and got to her feet. "You'll have to clear the room, and we need to secure the scene." She glanced to Bri. "You good with that, Inspector?"

Bri nodded, gently drawing Petra away and out of the small bedroom occupied by Lina's body. As she left, she made a final glance over the young woman she had been so desperate to find, the one she had wanted to find to give some sense of closure to Max's death—a death for which she couldn't help but partially blame herself.

Petra's hand, cool yet surprisingly strong, found its way into hers. Together, they stepped over the threshold.

50

It was what Trent would call a break in the weather, the day Lina and Max were laid to rest. After a lengthy search for any living relative, and coming up cold, the department took up a fund and, along with Petra's charitable connections, the pair were cremated together, their ashes placed into Bri's care. Vasily Sokolov, despite his many protests and assertations he could reveal the whereabouts to Korschev, was put into the hands of the FBI, who were also investigating their own Agent Kastner. Nothing had come of that either, as much as Bri had hoped to see justice for Lina and Max.

Andrei Korschev was on the run. Interpol had had several sightings of him, but nothing conclusive. Petra was constantly worried about her girls falling victim to the man, and she constantly reminded them to be vigilant.

Petra joined Bri on the bridge where she had first met with the witness who would eventually help lead them to Lina. Birds sang and the faint sound of San Francisco hummed in the background. Bri ran a finger over the silver box containing Lina and Max's ashes. It was only proper they should be laid to rest in such a peaceful place, having obtained special permission to do so. Maybe they would find in death the joy of the city, which they had never found in life.

Carefully, she opened the box, walking to a large tree, and gently spreading the ashes around the base. Pausing to say a silent word, Bri then rose and made her way back to the bridge, where Petra stood, her hair rippling in the breeze.

"Will you keep fighting?" Bri linked her fingers through Petra's as they looked out on the winter blossoms at the Botanical Gardens.

"Yes, every day." Petra squeezed her hand. "Every day."

INSPECTOR BRIANA RYU WILL RETURN IN CASTRO NIGHTS...

ACKNOWLEDGEMENTS

Briana Ryu is a character I've had in development for some time, but had kept very close to my heart. She is the culmination of years of writing experience, which finally encouraged me to bring her to life in the best way I possibly can.

Thanks as always go to my editor/bestie, Susie Watson, for unpicking all my mistakes and putting them back together again, checking for consistency, and commas and clichés (notes which I might still ignore).

Second, to one of my other best friends, Vince Laine. His support and encouragement kept me going during some of the rough patches. Lots of love!

To the awesome owners of Bearpig in Arbroath (James and Oleg). Thank you for letting me occupy your window seat on numerous days, typing like mad!

To Pavel Korzun, for his patience in helping me find the right Russian words to use, and for putting up with my constant, "Wait, I have one more!"

To my beta readers, who, once again, convinced me this book is worth publishing.

To my readers. Without you, I am nothing.

To my son for, again, his timeless patience.

To my partner for giving in to my pleadings to PLEASE read my book and tell me it's good.

Finally, to all my friends and family. Thank you for believing in me. This one's for you, Grandpa! Love and miss you.

ABOUT THE AUTHOR

Heather Osborne, an author of crime and historical novels, was born and raised in California. She has a Bachelor of Science in Criminology and Victimology. In 2009, she moved to Scotland. Along with her novels and short stories, Heather also has written and directed several plays. In her spare time, she enjoys reading, writing (of course!), and theatre, as well as caring for her young son. Among her published titles are: The Soldier's Secret, a historical romance set during the American Civil War; Bitter Bonds, a tale of black magic in the deep South in the 1840s; and the Rae Hatting Mysteries series.

Find her at: www.heatherosborneauthor.com

Printed in Poland
by Amazon Fulfillment
Poland Sp. z o.o., Wrocław